BURNING BED (SPECIAL FORCES: OPERATION ALPHA)

AIR FORCE FIRE PROTECTION SPECIALISTS BOOK 6

JEN TALTY

This book is a work of fiction. Names, characters, places, and incidents are products of the author's imagination or used fictitiously. Any resemblance to actual events or locales or persons living or dead is entirely coincidental.

Dear Readers,

Welcome to the Special Forces: Operation Alpha Fan-Fiction world!

If you are new to this amazing world, in a nutshell the author wrote a story using one or more of my characters in it. Sometimes that character has a major role in the story, and other times they are only mentioned briefly. This is perfectly legal and allowable because they are going through Aces Press to publish the story.

This book is entirely the work of the author who wrote it. While I might have assisted with brainstorming and other ideas about which of my characters to use, I didn't have any part in the process or writing or editing the story.

I'm proud and excited that so many authors loved my characters enough that they wanted to write them into their own story. Thank you for supporting them, and me!

READ ON!

Xoxo

Susan Stoker

To Kimberly Dawn. Thanks for going the extra mile!

CHAPTER 1

"How'd you get so lucky to live next to someone who looks like that? She's smoking hot."

Senior Firefighter Garret Peirce wouldn't argue that point with his co-worker, Zach Santora, as he pointed to Garret's sexy neighbor who unfortunately had been giving him the cold shoulder lately.

"Put your testosterone in your pocket. She's way out of your league," Garret said, taking the turn into his driveway a little too fast. The last conversation he'd had with Tabitha Nelson had gone worse than the first time he tried to kiss a girl and he missed her lips and got her nose.

It was not a good kiss, to say the least.

"Oh, she's in my league all right, but the question is why haven't you asked her out yet?" Zach asked.

Garret and Zach had been working together for close to ten years. They had started off as junior firemen when almost all of the Fire Protection Specialist Team he'd been assigned to had been single. Now, about half were married, and collectively they had eleven kids.

That's more than a kid a year.

Garret wouldn't mind adding to that number someday in the near future. Zach often teased him about his desire to settle down and yet, since they've known each other, Garret had had only four girlfriends, and none of them lasted more than a year.

Zach, on the other hand, wanted nothing to do with long-term relationships, much less having a family. Only two years younger than Garret, he had plenty of time to change his tune on that.

Garret, however, at thirty, was looking for the right woman to settle down with and have a bunch of little rug-rats. Hell, he'd even resorted to babysitting for some of his buddies because he loved kids that much. His mother joked that he had a biological clock that taunted him as it ticked away in the back of his heart.

His mother was right.

"Why don't you mind your own business." He slammed the truck into park, doing his best to avoid the glare of his neighbor. They'd only been neighbors for a couple of months since he'd recently moved from an apartment to this house, and he thought they had hit it off.

Well, as best he could with a beautiful, smart woman that had the kind of confidence most people strived for, but never achieved. The first time they talked at any length one morning by the garbage cans, not three minutes into the conversation, Garret had not only become enamored by her, but intimidated as well. It had been her who initiated their first date, if you could call a stroll around the block a date.

After a few evenings of walks and the occasional drink on one of their back patios, he'd gotten up the nerve to ask her out on a real date.

Then her brother died the following day. That had been two weeks ago, and he'd done what he could to offer support, but it wasn't the time or place to pursue a romantic relationship. He figured that could wait until she'd had some time to get through the shock.

Five days ago, she had shown up on his doorstep, asking if he could take a look at the report she'd been given regarding the fire.

She didn't like his answer, and she'd barely spoken to him since.

Garret glanced in his rearview mirror as his buddies, Noah and Gunner, the EMTs, parked their car on the street.

Noah had been with the team for five years and Gunner six. Both good men.

Carter and Mason, the newest and youngest firefighters, having only been with the team for the last year, should be pulling in any second.

The team had just gotten off a twenty-four-hour shift. In the last year, the single men on the team had developed a habit of coming back to Garret's rented house near the beach for breakfast. They'd hang out and unwind for an hour or so, enjoying the warm ocean breeze.

Garret snagged one of the bags filled with breakfast sandwiches from the back seat since it had been his turn to pick up the tab.

"Because I'm the dude that has your back."

"She's had a tough time. Can't be easy to have lost your parents to a car accident and then a few years later, your brother to a fire." Garret cringed. He'd tried to lend her an ear and a helping hand.

But she wanted someone to tell her that she was right. That someone had killed her brother. Not that all the evidence showed that her brother died after a fire had been started in his bedroom after he'd shot drugs into his veins.

She didn't want to believe her brother had fallen off the wagon. He could understand that, however, the autopsy showed more than one drug in his system. Going through life with blinders on about her sibling wasn't doing her any favors. The evidence that Garret had seen was indisputable.

And he told her as much, which meant he'd probably never get a second chance to even have one date.

"What does that have to do with you and her between the sheets?" Zach closed the truck door and carried a couple of trays of coffee and soft drinks. "And if you're not going to tap that, then step out of the way for me."

"That doesn't sound like a man who has my back. Maybe a man who would stab me in the back." Garret glanced over his shoulder, stepping onto the back patio. Tabitha stood in her side yard, watering her plants as she did every morning. Her frayed jean shorts hugged her slender hips and round ass. She wore a white tank top, and her shoulder-length, dark hair brushed against her bare shoulders. A sexy tattoo dotted her right shoulder. It was of a half-moon and the side of a woman's face where the hair reached around the moon as if they were arms. She'd said it had to do with having overly vivid dreams. Whatever the inspiration, the tatt had to be one of the coolest ones he'd seen on a woman's body.

He waved with his free hand, but she just turned her head.

Like she had ever since she'd asked him if he could look into the fire report that had killed her brother.

"Are you dating her?" Zach asked.

Garret shook his head.

"Then watch a real man at work." Zach set the tray on the patio table before Garret could warn him. Then again, it might be fun to see Zach come running back with his tail between his legs. Didn't happen often, so this would be a real treat because no way would Tabitha ever say yes to a guy like Zach. She was too smart not to see through his charm. It was too bad, because Zach really was a good man; he just couldn't stay with a lady longer than a couple of months. And even that might be pushing it.

Garret did his best not to stare as he watched his buddy approach Tabitha. She barely smiled but glanced in Garret's direction with narrowed eyes.

He shrugged, wishing he could hear the conversation, but as soon as Tabitha waved her one hand dismissively, Garret knew the conversation had abruptly ended.

Zach turned, stuffing his hands deep in his pockets, sporting a scowl just as the rest of their buddies stepped into the backyard.

"Did he just go hit on your neighbor?" Mason asked, slapping Garret on the back. Mason wasn't even twenty-five yet, but he had an old soul with a wicked sense of humor. "That's rude considering you had wanted to first. Did she turn you down? Or did you just never get up the nerve? Really, I have no idea why you're so shy. You're tall, okay, maybe a little too tall, but if I were gay, I'd be interested."

Garret laughed, shaking his head. "You're too short." At a little over six four, he struggled to date any woman under five nine. Tabitha had to be close, give or take a half-inch. "I had more than a chance had I told her the cops and fire investigator were wrong about her brother, but when I couldn't do that, she pushed me away."

"Shit, I forgot about her brother." Mason shook his head. "That really sucks."

Garret decided to turn his attention to Zach who scuffed his feet on the concrete patio. Zach didn't believe there wasn't a woman he couldn't get in the sack. So, to watch Tabitha blow him off was a tad more enjoyable than it should be. "What did she say?" Garret asked.

"That I wasn't her type." Zach rolled his eyes. "Something about not being tall enough."

"Har har, you're a funny guy." Zach might be six foot on a good day, but Garret knew Tabitha hadn't cut him off at the pass based on his height. Garret caught Tabitha's gaze. She paused, holding the hose over her rose garden. She tilted her head and if he wasn't mistaken, her lips curved. It wasn't a scowl, nor was it even a hint of a smile.

More of an acknowledgement that at one time, they had the beginning of something sweet, but her focus now was solely on proving someone killed her brother. Until she did that, there would be no room for Garret.

Or anyone else.

"I heard she told a reporter that her brother said he was working on a story and that if something happened to him, it wouldn't have been an accident," Gunner pulled back one of the chairs, taking a coffee and pulling off the top, Mason following suit.

"I heard her brother didn't even have a job."

Noah opened the bag, emptying the contents on the table. "How could he be working on anything?"

Garret focused on the smell of bacon, cheese, and sausage filling the air, reminding him it had been at least four hours since he'd had a single bite to eat, ignoring the chatter about Steve, Tabitha's brother. He'd gotten a lot of bad press that wasn't entirely accurate. "That's not true."

The sound of a car in serious need of a new muffler echoed down the street before stopping in front of Garret's driveway. Carter's truck always needed work, and everyone thought he should replace it. Even though he was only twenty-three, he could afford a new one, or at the very least to fix the damn thing.

"He wrote articles for online magazines and worked part-time for a local television station," Garret corrected. While Steve didn't make a lot of money, he did work, and his goal had been to work as an investigative reporter for a major news program.

At least that is what Tabitha had told him.

Garret had never met Steve and had no idea what he had really been like, but it did seem odd that a thirty-two-year-old man had yet to carve out his career, and he had a past criminal record for possession and the sale of illegal drugs.

"What I'd miss?" Carter asked as he strolled into the backyard with his blond hair perfectly styled in something he described as an edgy undercut with it trimmed short on the sides, but long on the top.

"We were just discussing the lack of Garret's love life and the object of his affection's brother," Zach said, turning a chair and straddling it with a shitty-ass grin.

"Before I left my house—"

Gunner interrupted Carter. "Why do you always go home and shower? We smell your stench all damn day at the station. So why take the time when we're all still covered in soot?"

"I like to be clean before I eat breakfast." Carter snatched a sandwich, tossing it in the air before settling on the steps that led to the kitchen. "As I was saying, while I was getting dressed, the morning news interviewed the chief of police about her accusations that someone planted the drugs in her brother's house. He said there is no reason to believe that any foul play had been involved in the case. Then they brought up some old charges from a few years ago."

"Tabitha said he'd been clean and sober for the

last few years." Garret took one of the cups of coffee and pulled off the top, inhaling the rich aroma of the best morning brew known to man. "She brought over the report from both the fire department and the police, and I couldn't find anything that seemed out of the ordinary, but she's not going to stop until someone listens."

"And you think she's wrong?" Noah asked, leaning back and folding his arms. He always enjoyed playing the devil's advocate.

"I honestly don't know," Garret admitted.

"What about the autopsy report?" Gunner asked.

"Says he was jacked up on heroin and ecstasy. The fire was started in the bedroom by a candle. No accelerant of any kind had been used. Case closed."

"Then maybe she's going to need to let it go and accept her brother was using drugs," Zach said. "It sucks, but it's reality."

Garret watched Tabitha as she coiled the hose and carried it toward the garage. She used to have a bounce to her walk and a twinkle in her eye. All she had now was slumped shoulders and a deep sadness lined with a ring of fire filled with anger. She pulled her cell phone from her back pocket.

Two seconds later, his buzzed.

TABITHA: WHEN YOUR FRIENDS LEAVE, COULD YOU STOP by? I won't take but ten minutes of your time.

HE SUCKED IN A DEEP BREATH, TAKING THE SALTY AIR deep in his lungs before letting it out slowly. He lived only one block from the beach because of the ocean breeze and the sounds of the waves crashing against the sandy shore. There was nothing more calming than the blue waters of the sea.

GARRET: SURE THING. IT WILL BE ABOUT AN HOUR. IS that okay? I could come over now if necessary.

WHAT THE HELL DID HE MEAN BY *NECESSARY*? WHAT A dumb fucking word to use. She probably just wanted to ream him out for letting his buddy go hit on her, and considering all that she had been through, that had been an asshole move on his part. Though, he couldn't have stopped Zach if he'd tried.

TABITHA: NO. ENJOY YOUR FRIENDS. I'M WORKING FROM home today, so whenever.

Garret: OK. Won't be too long.

HE TUCKED HIS PHONE BACK IN HIS POCKET AND snagged an egg sandwich. He didn't care if it had sausage, turkey sausage, or bacon, as long as it filled his stomach and got his mind off his neighbor.

Her dead brother.

And the fire that had killed him.

CHAPTER 2

Tabitha found herself sitting in her living room, staring out the window, waiting for all of Garret's friends to scatter. They all seemed like nice enough men, even Zach, whose reputation preceded him. It had surprised her that he'd come over to give his condolences and then to ask her to give Garret a break and go out on a date with him.

Which meant that Garret hadn't ever discussed their time together, much less what she'd asked of him. Or if he did, Zach was a nicer guy than any woman had ever given him credit for.

The last one of Garret's friends climbed in their vehicle and drove off.

Her pulse soared like a peak reaching toward the bright-blue sky poking through a thick layer of clouds that hid the sun. Right now, she resented how the tall, muscular, sexy fireman made her want to forget her troubles in his strong arms for a night of what she knew would be more thrilling than the first time she parasailed off the top of a mountain in the Alps.

But she couldn't let her brother's death be in vain. She would finish what he started, even if it was the last thing she did.

Ding. Dong.

She jumped up from the sofa, adjusting her top as she tried to take her time answering the door. Garret had a way of making her feel like a seventeen-year-old girl, not a twenty-eight-year-old woman. His quiet, shy demeanor only added to the allure. He was the kind of man that you just knew, once you got past his awkwardness, would be a passionate and adoring lover. He would be the kind of boyfriend that when he gave his heart, it would yours forever.

And the kind of man that could steal hers with a mere glance.

Opening the door, she plastered on her best smile. "Thanks for coming over. I appreciate it."

"My pleasure. What do you need?" He rubbed at his tired, dark-russet eyes. His five-o'clock shadow in full spicy-scruff mode made his face seem innocent with a touch of a sweet devil.

She could only imagine what it would be like to have to work a twenty-four-hour shift. She could barely work ten hours in a day without falling over from exhaustion. "I need you to look at two things for me."

"Okay."

She turned to avoid giving him the once-over, but she found it impossible not to look. His shoulders weren't overly broad, but they were well-defined. His biceps bulged through his white T-shirt and oh, how his jeans hung on his hips. A tad baggy, but she could still see the definition in his thigh muscles.

Not to mention his tight ass.

Sculptors used his body for inspiration.

"Where are we going?" he asked as she stepped into her family room.

"I want you to look at my back door and tell me if you think someone might have tried to break in." She leaned against the counter and folded her arms, knowing she was closing herself off. Her attraction to him only got in the way. Besides, he didn't believe her.

So, why had she asked him over?

He stood two feet from her, hands on his hips, staring. "Why do you think that?" His tone was neither aggressive, nor sensitive.

If anything, it was indifferent.

"I thought I heard something last night in the backyard. I turned on all the lights and called the cops, who did nothing, of course. But when I opened the door this morning, it looked damaged."

"What did the police say?"

"They walked around the yard and inside the house. They also took a report and said it was possible that someone tried to jimmy the door, but they found no other evidence." While they had said all that, the one cop looked at her like she had ten heads. When she asked if they could dust for prints, he practically rolled his eyes. However, his partner did so, just in case, but said since the house was fifty years old, the damage could be wear and tear. That said, the door itself couldn't be more than ten years old and the lock about the same.

"All right. Let me look." Garret lowered himself to the floor and examined the lock. His long fingers ran across the wood. His biceps flexed with his effortless movement. He concentrated on that door almost as well as she concentrated on every inch of his body.

She found herself biting down on her fingernail and letting out an audible sigh. Her body even shuddered with a warm tingle going places that, thankfully, he couldn't see.

He glanced over his shoulder. "Can you get me a screwdriver, both flat and Phillips head?"

"No problem." She padded around the kitchen counter to the closet by the garage door and pulled out a small toolkit. With shaky fingers, she set it on the floor. "I think that should have everything you need."

He nodded, flipping open the top. "You're the owner, right?"

"Yes." She narrowed her eyes, glancing over his shoulder as he unscrewed the plate on the side of the door. "Why?"

He pressed into the frayed wood. "It's not rotted and based on looking at the back side, I'd say someone tried to pry the door open, so now it's been weakened." He quickly put the plate back on and stood, reaching out, pressing his large hand against the wall. "I'd replace the entire thing. It's a standard door, so I'm sure a place like Home Repairs has it."

"But you think someone could have tried to break in?" She desperately needed one person to believe her.

"It's possible, but it doesn't mean it happened last night. It could have been before you bought the house. But even so, there have been a couple of break-ins in the neighborhood. Why don't you have a deadbolt? This doorknob lock is useless."

She shrugged. "I kept saying I'd get a new lock. Just never did."

"You said you're working from home today?"

She nodded, trying to keep the drool from dripping out of the corner of her mouth. She wanted to reach up and run her fingertips over the day-old growth on the sides of his face. Most mornings, she'd see him all clean-shaven, which gave him a sophisticated rich boy look like he should be leaning against a private jet in a power suit.

However, she preferred the outdoorsy type, and the man standing in front of her now should be wearing a flannel shirt, unbuttoned, and riding a horse.

"I plan on it, unless something happens, and I have to go out."

"Perfect. I'll go get the right door and a much better lock. Have you considered putting in a couple of security cameras?"

She shook her head, letting her mind drift from

doing the dirty with Mr. Hot Buns to the second reason she'd wanted him to stop by.

"They are easy to install, and you can control them from an app on your phone. Do you want me to get that done today as well?" He pushed off the wall and rested his ass against the counter, leaning back and crossing his ankles. He had a few wrinkles around the eyes and a scar on the bottom of the chin, and those slight imperfections made him even more decadent.

"I don't want to put you out. Besides you must be exhausted, so I can hire—"

"It will be weeks before you'll get a handyman out here. I've got nothing going on, so no biggie, and I promise my fee will be really low."

She arched a brow. "And what might that be?"

He scratched the side of his head. His light-brown hair flowed a little over his ear, but he normally kept his hair short on the sides, a smidgen longer on top, and it was always a little messy, like someone had ran their fingers through the strands and ruffled them.

"For the door? Dinner would work. And for the lock and deadbolt, I think a nice bottle of wine would be good payment."

She laughed. "And for the security cameras?"

"A stroll to Timmy's Treats for some ice cream, since this will probably take a few hours."

"It's a deal," she said, shoving out her hand. Though she should have thought about it and then made him put a dollar value on the work, but then she figured they could talk about the things she found on the computer.

"You mentioned there were two things you wanted to show me?"

If she told him now, he might get pissed and walk out of her house, not helping her with the door. "We can talk about that over dinner."

"Sounds good." He rested his hands on her shoulders, massaging gently.

Oh, how she wanted to feel those fingers digging into her flesh.

Sucking in a slow breath, she filled her lungs with what smelled like crisp air on top of a mountain on a foggy day with a slight drizzle trickling from the hazy sky. "I really appreciate the help."

"It's the least I can do for letting my idiot friend come over and hit on you."

She tilted her head. "That's what he said? Because all he did was give me his condolences for my brother."

Garret licked his full lips. She stared as his

tongue slowly glided over the plump flesh. "Zach can be a good guy when he wants to be."

"He took out a friend of mine once. It didn't end well for her. You know, I'll call you later, never calls, and then she finds out he's dating some girl she works with."

"He's going to run out of women willing to date him."

Without thinking too much about how her actions could be taken, she looped her arms around his middle. His tight muscles twitched under her touch. "I'm sorry I got so mad at you when all you've ever done is help me. But I think after you read something I found on my brother's computer, you might think like I do."

He drew his lips into a tight line. "I know you're hurting, but—"

"Just read it. That's all I ask." She held her breath, staring into his dreamy, rich mocha orbs that reminded her of the river of chocolate in the movie *Willie Wonka and the Chocolate Factory,* and she wanted to jump in naked for a nice, warm bath, letting him coat her skin.

"I'm really sorry about what happened to your brother, and I'm here for you if you need anything, so yes, I'll read it. But don't expect me to give you the answers you want to hear. I won't do that. I will, however, always be honest with my opinion."

She dropped her forehead to his firm chest, focusing on the rise and fall of his breath. "My brother was a lot of things, drug addict included, but I told you he was worried something might happen to him."

"That could be paranoia caused by drug use."

"I know it could be, but I know my brother and he wasn't using the last time I saw him."

His hands ran up and down her arms before he gripped her forearms, taking a step back. "I read those reports three times. There is nothing hinky about them."

"But did you talk to—"

"I'm going to go get my tools, take some measurements, and head to the store. We can talk about this tonight."

"I'd rather pay you cash. You're going to side with your own and not consider the possibility that maybe someone in the local police or fire department, or even higher up could be corrupt and capable—"

"Trust me. I know some bad people in my profession. One of my own tried to kill my buddy Brodie and his wife, so don't you dare make that assumption of me. I looked at everything you asked me to with a watchful eye. I tried to find foul play, but it's just not there. Now, excuse me while I take care of your door, and then I'll read whatever it is, and I'll treat it the same way I did the last time." He let out a big huff before turning and stomping out of the kitchen. "I won't take your money, but I will need to eat."

She clenched her fists, then shook them out with a violent whip of her wrists. The media had made a mockery of her brother's death the second she started questioning the reports. They dug up every wrongdoing he'd ever been caught in but didn't once look at the good things he'd done, or how he'd begun to turn his life around.

He didn't overdose on drugs and accidentally burn his house down.

And she was going to prove it with or without Garret's help.

CHAPTER 3

"Thank you. That was delicious." Garret pushed his plate to the side while Tabitha shoved a laptop in his face. She'd been sitting across from him through the entire dinner, tapping her foot erratically on the tile floor. He'd barely had a chance to enjoy the penne pasta with a white cream sauce and some chicken.

Her cooking was about as good as going home just for his mom's cuisine.

"Glad you liked it." She snagged the plate, nearly dropping the utensils on his lap. She'd barely spoken and when she did, it was like little daggers were being shot out of her mouth and stabbing him in the heart.

"What am I looking at?" He could only imagine the grief she must be experiencing. In a way, he understood why she'd pushed herself to believe her brother had been murdered. She'd mentioned to him more than once how proud she'd been that he was finally moving forward with his life.

But often, people fell back on old, bad habits, and her brother had been a bit of a deadbeat with no real goals for a long time.

At least according to the stories she'd told him.

"Some of my brother's notes I found on his laptop. The weird thing is, it starts out as a letter to me." He glanced over the screen, catching a glimpse of her backside while she did the dishes. Her round hips filled out her mini-skirt and her legs, damn they went on forever.

But it wasn't only her pretty face and hot body that Garret liked. Tabitha could hold her end of an intelligent conversation. She had to be the smartest person in any room.

And kind.

He'd watched her on more than one occasion go out of her way to help a neighbor. She had a heart of gold.

But she also had the kind of sheer determination that once she went after something, she'd never let go, and in the case of her brother, she was going to need to find a way to move past all this.

The least he could do was look at the documents.

Tabitha,

If you're reading this, then a couple of things happened. You looked under your bed, which you never do, not even to clean, and found my laptop, and I'm still alive and we might laugh over this.

Or not.

Or. I'm injured, and I told you about the laptop.

Or, more than likely, I'm dead and you do what you always do when you're upset, you clean.

"You don't clean under your bed?" He lifted his eyelids.

"That's what you're focusing on?"

He shook his head. "No. I'm asking because of what your brother said about what you do when you're upset."

"My garage is spotless, every closet has been organized, and my bathrooms have never been cleaner, but I hadn't gotten to moving furniture and cleaning under it." She cocked her head. "Read on."

It starts with the incident at Ivan Moore's residence, a local businessman. He resides on Windjammer Point which is located on Merritt Island. I've been to the house when I was dating Ashley, who is friends with his daughter, but I only met the man in passing. I didn't have any real contact with him.

It was suspected a few years back that Ivan Moore was involved in securities fraud and embezzlement. That accusation seems to have disappeared about a year after his son-in-law became an Assistant District Attorney.

A year ago, the police were called to the residence during a party when my ex-girlfriend took ill. The story is that Ashley Hanover died of anaphylactic shock after consuming a dish she was unaware had peanuts, and she'd forgotten her EpiPen that evening.

I call bullshit. Ashley never went anywhere without that thing and the Moore's knew about her allergies. She was also deathly allergic to shellfish and bee stings.

"You didn't tell me any of this when your brother died." Actually, all she had said when her brother died was that someone killed him because he didn't do drugs, so no way could he have overdosed. Nothing about the party, or his friend.

Tabitha waved a bottle of wine.

He nodded.

"I didn't know anything about this until I found his laptop under my bed this morning."

"When the hell did he put it there and why?" he asked, taking the glass of red wine she offered. He swirled the rich liquid, letting it hug the sides before taking a long sniff. The thick, rich, dry scent hit his nostrils with the force of a gust of wind. Nothing beat a nice Cab.

"I assumed when he came by two days before he died, telling me if anything happened to him, it wouldn't have been an accident." She sat next to him, setting the bottle on the table. "I only saw it because I finally got to cleaning under my bed." Her sarcastic tone wasn't lost on him.

"What was she doing at Moore's house the day she died?"

"First, she's good friends with his daughter Lisa, according to Steve. And she worked for Mr. Moore for a couple of summers. My guess is that she was helping my brother with this story."

"He's been working on it for over a year?"

"I guess. I mean, he's been writing articles for the last eighteen months, and he's told me in the past, that some took months and months to collect all the information needed to make it so the editor would accept it. The last time I talked to him, he had five stories on his desk."

"Sounds like a hard way to make a living." Garret rolled his neck. "So, your brother thought they put peanuts in her food intentionally?"

"That's the thought."

"But why?"

"Not exactly sure, but it gets better. Keep reading." With a delicate touch of her finger, she smoothed a strand of hair behind her ears as she raised one leg, resting her heel on the chair, hugging her knee with one hand, holding a flute of wine in the other.

He turned his attention back to the computer screen.

I MANAGED TO SNAG AN INTERVIEW WITH SANDRA Creeco about six months ago. She was the receptionist at Moore Industries. She had also attended the party the night Ashley died. She had told Ashley to back off the digging and poking into Moore's business dealings. That she was going to get herself in trouble. After Ashley died, Sandra became more suspicious and started looking for information on her own, keeping me in the loop.

She was killed in a freak car accident three days after

she contacted me letting me know she found something. Said she was going to either bring it by, or maybe mail it to me.

I have no idea what that something was. I never got it. I tried going to her house, but her roommate wouldn't let me in. Slammed the door in my face. She won't take my calls. I'm concerned for her safety if she has anything or knows anything.

However, Sandra had managed to get me a list of names from the party.

I got a hold of a junior associate, Eddy Green. He had nothing to say. Nor did a copywriter named Finn Tor and of course, Moore, his daughter, or Lisa's husband, Jeff Bellen, the Assistant District Attorney, wouldn't speak to me.

The day I after I spoke to both Finn and Eddy, someone broke into my home. I don't know how they got in, but my desk had been ransacked. All the drawers open. Papers missing. Thankfully, my computer goes with me wherever I go, and I hadn't left one piece of paper regarding Ashley or my thoughts on how she died.

The cops did nothing. Officer Riley and Dani had been the ones who arrived about ten minutes after I called. They dusted for prints. But found no forced entry anywhere and asked if maybe an ex-girlfriend or someone with a key could have come in and did this out of spite.

Yeah. Probably Moore, since I suspect he's the one who made sure there were peanuts in Ashley's food, but I didn't say that, and he didn't have a key, obviously.

Though Ashley had one.

I made more phone calls to the people on the list from the party, but no one would talk to me.

A couple of weeks ago, I got a phone call from Kelly Rines, that's Sandra's roommate. She said she found something and would bring it to me. I met her at a diner, and she gave me a folder. Inside were copies of ledgers and billings that didn't seem to add up. Ashley had made notes, showing all the discrepancies, but what jumped out at her had been a company named HCV Limited, a heating and cooling company owned by Rocco Tias, a known drug dealer, who had just recently been arrested and then two days later, his case tossed out on a technicality. I did a quick search, and he's been arrested four times in the last two years, all tossed out.

That seems odd.

Then I got a message in my email. It came from JB0857@aol.com. I have no idea who that is and thus far, I haven't been able to figure it out.

Here is the email, for the record:

I strongly urge you to back off your investigative

piece into Ivan Moore. If you don't, you're putting yourself in grave danger. You'll understand in due time.

I have to say, that's an oddly worded threat, however, it's a threat nonetheless.

In this folder, I have scanned all the documents.

Tabitha, I wouldn't take this to the local police. Or the District Attorney's office. Take it to someone you trust. Someone who might have connections. And then walk away. Don't look back.

Love,

Your pain in the ass little brother.

"THAT'S A LOT TO TAKE IN," GARRET SAID.

"And it doesn't sound like its coming from a man addicted to heroin, does it?"

He nodded. No arguing that point.

Garret clicked on the scanned PDF with all the handwritten notes, then looked at the email.

He lowered the top of the computer. "Do you know if he talked to anyone else about all this?"

"No idea," she said.

"You said he was here two days before he died. What exactly did he tell you?"

"He thought someone was following him. When I asked him why, he said he couldn't tell me, but to watch my back and of course, that ominous statement about if something happened to him, it wouldn't be an accident."

Garret pushed back his chair, took his wine, and moved across the room, knowing she might actually toss something at him for his next question. "Is it possible he was on something? Was he acting unusually paranoid?"

"Not on something, but definitely paranoid," she said behind gritted teeth. "He was freaked out."

"Then why didn't he tell you about all this stuff?"

"I'm thinking he wanted to protect me. Hell, two people are dead."

That didn't make for murder, but he'd keep that thought to himself. "When he came over that day, did he have a bag? Did you see him go into your room?"

She shook her head. "We sat outside. He was always looking over his shoulder, and every time he heard a car, he jumped. He didn't go in the house."

Garret arched a brow. "Then how the hell did that," he pointed to the computer, "get under your bed?"

"My brother had a set of keys. He could have put it there anytime."

"Well, at least we changed the lock on the back

door." He glanced at his watch. "The hardware store is still open. I can run down and get a new lock for the front door tonight."

"You don't have to do that, but does it mean you believe me?"

"To be frank, I don't know what I believe. Your brother has gotten some bad press and some of it is true. An autopsy doesn't lie, and the evidence is pretty damning with the amount of drugs they found in his body and in his house."

Her eyes narrowed to tiny, little slits as she opened her mouth.

He wasn't about to let her ream him out again.

"Let me finish. Even if all the stuff about your brother is true, it doesn't change the documents he has that clearly point out some miscalculations with Moore's business and the ties between the two dead girls. We'll need to call someone to help us figure this out."

"Are you nuts? We call the cops, and we're both probably dead."

He bit his tongue. Part of him knew there was something to the information, but it was above his pay grade, and he didn't want to upset her any more than she already was. "A friend of mine that I grew up with, her husband is Delta Force and his connections reach far and wide. I'd like to call him and forward this information to him. He doesn't have any skin in this game, he'll be impartial, and dig where no one else can."

"Oh. I see." She gulped her wine. "By all means. Thank you."

Closing the gap, he rested his hand on her shoulder. "I need you to promise me two things if I'm going to ask my buddies to help me poke into this."

"What's that?"

He held up his index finger. "First, you will stay out of it. No detective work on your part at all. If even a little bit of what you say is true, or what your brother thought happened to his friend, then you could be next."

She opened her mouth, but he pinched it closed with his fingers, leaning over. "And second, if something weird happens, or you think someone is watching you, anything, you call me straight away, day or night. Got it?" He dropped his hand to his side.

"I can live with that."

"Good. Want to come with me to the store and pick out the kind of lock you want?"

"Actually, I like the one you got for the back door, can you just pick up something like that?"

"Sure, but make sure you lock the door. I'll be back in a half hour."

He stepped outside and let his mind go over the documents he'd scanned on Steve's computer. He had to admit, the paperwork looked fishy, but they were talking white-collar crimes. The addition of Rocco Tias, well that made murder less of a stretch.

But the lead fire investigator for the fire at her brother's house had been Wesley Armond, a former Fire Protection Specialist for the Air Force.

No way would he compromise evidence.

So, where did that leave Garret and his quest to help Tabitha find the answers she wanted?

He let out a long breath. Talk about a lose-lose situation.

CHAPTER 4

Garret twisted the deadbolt, satisfied the front door would be secure. He handed Tabitha two keys. "Keep it locked, and don't leave the spare key outside anywhere. That's just asking for trouble."

She snagged them from his hand, smacking him so hard it stung. "I never have, and I wouldn't start now." Her feet scuffed as she crossed the foyer, making a loud clicking noise with her sandals.

He followed her into the kitchen, watching her open a cabinet, tossing one of the keys in a bowl. She turned and leaned against the counter with her hands folded across her chest.

"Are you mad at me?" His inability to understand women and their moods had to be one of the biggest reasons he behaved like a moron around them.

Not to mention why he didn't have a girlfriend.

However, he normally didn't ask such questions, partly because he didn't know why and partly because he wasn't sure it was worth making an ass of himself.

Everything was potential embarrassment when it came to Tabitha, and he wasn't going to screw up a chance with her just because he couldn't string together an intelligent conversation with a woman unless it had to do with firefighting, the Air Force, or trucks.

"Ya think?" She cocked her head and smiled at him with a sarcastic grin. "What gave it away?"

"Oh, I don't know, maybe it's the way you shuffled across the floor like a kid who just got scolded and now you're being—"

"I'd stop right there if I were you," she said, running her fingers through her shiny, dark hair. The strands flopped back over her shoulders. "It would serve you better to take a step back, think about why I might be mad, and address that, instead of mocking me."

He positioned himself next to her, his hip rubbing gently against hers. "I don't mean to mock, so I'm sorry about that. But you went from let's have a drink to slamming cabinet doors like I insulted you...oh." The lightbulb went off in his head. "You didn't like me telling you not to leave a key outside."

"Bingo."

"I was just looking out for your safety. Honestly, it's a hazard of the job. My mom gets pissed when I come home and immediately check all her fire detectors." He glanced to the ceiling, looking at hers.

"Want to test it?"

He shook his head.

She let out a long breath. "Have you heard anything?"

"I'm waiting for my buddy, Fletch, to get back to me. I gave him the list of players and as I told you, he's got friends in high places, and a few low places. If there is something to find, he and his buddies at Delta Force will find it. I also contacted Harper. I don't know if you ever met Brodie, but she's his wife. She's an Air Force investigator. She's got a million more resources than I do. Until we hear back from them, I think you should act as if you've accepted what happened to your brother—"

"But I haven't accepted it, and I won't."

He pressed his finger over her warm, plump lips, resisting the urge to trace their outline then slip his tongue between them. He'd felt desire before. He'd seen a woman and wanted her so bad he'd trip over his tongue a dozen times trying to get her into his bedroom.

But never had a woman had him seeing a future filled with a life of love and happiness. The more he got to know Tabitha, the more he knew deep down, she was the kind of person he wanted to be with.

And that included her directness and sarcasm.

"If someone tried to break into your house, and if someone did murder your brother, then it's only going to make whoever is behind this come at you harder. If they think you have something on them, then you could end up like your brother." He looped his arms behind her back and tugged her from the counter. With both hands gripping her waist, he stared intently into her captivating, but questioning eyes. "I don't want anything to happen to you, and looking at what your brother has on his computer, it's got me on high alert."

"Once again, I ask, do you believe me?"

He blinked his eyes closed for a long moment while he took a deep, cleansing breath. "Without a doubt, I know it's what you believe. I deal in facts and right now, the facts surrounding your brother's death are pretty solid." Before she could open her pretty, little mouth and spout off a dozen defenses, he swiped his lips across hers in a swift, but powerful kiss. "But what's on your brother's computer is disturbing and absolutely worth exploring. Only you need to leave the probing to me."

She cocked her head in that confident demeanor she always had, and he adored that about her. She went through her day as if there wasn't anything she couldn't tackle. It had been one of the first things he noticed about her the day they met at a neighborhood block party.

"Probing?" she asked with a laugh. "Did you really just say that?"

He really needed to learn to hear how things sounded in his head before he opened his mouth in front of a woman.

"Look into?"

"That's less sexual, but honestly, I'm a big girl and can take care of myself."

"That I don't doubt. Not for one single second. But I think in this case, it's best to think as though we're dealing with hardened criminals, and neither one of us are equipped to deal with them."

"But you're in the Air Force. I'd say you're *equipped* to deal with just about anything." Her hands landed on his shoulders, rubbing gently, sending a message to the rest of his body that maybe he hadn't crashed and burned.

Yet.

"I'm pretty good with a weapon, but the only missions I've ever been on have been related to fighting fires. Might be dangerous, but my weapon of choice is a hose filled with—"

"Oh. My. God. Stop before I pee my pants."

"I was going to say water. You know, the substance that is used to put out things that are burning."

"My mind is still going to the down and dirty." Her chest heaved with an intake of breath, pressing against his in a sensual act he had a hard time ignoring. He should discount any pretense of sexual aggression on her part.

Or on his, for that matter.

Things had taken an odd turn with them the day her brother died.

And there was the grief that still had to swell in her heart. He'd seen it the day he'd gone to the wake and stood in that line, waiting to express his deepest condolences. She'd been distracted that day, which he had anticipated. He certainly didn't expect her to spend any time with him. But she had cornered him with her questions and accusations, then demanded his help.

"You're just using it to avoid the subject. I know you want to push the cops—"

"You don't think that me talking to anyone who is willing to listen will get people in power to reopen the case?"

"I know it won't." He curled his fingers together behind her back, pulling her closer. "It will put them on the defensive, and they will find every negative thing they can dig up on you, your brother, and anyone else you love, making it their mission to destroy you. It will become a shitstorm that will hurt you in ways you might not recover from. I fear you've already done some damage with how vocal you've been." Her body molded against his as if he were the sand and she were the ocean waves, rolling in, taking little pieces of him, only to bring them back with another kiss.

"You think I should just hush my mouth. Walk away with my tail between my legs. Let my brother's death be in vain."

"You know that's not what I'm saying. I'm trying to protect you *and* help you. Why are making this so difficult? I'm on your side."

"I want to believe you, but you know the fire investigator and you know some of the cops—"

"If what you say is true, this happened long

before the first responders showed up on the scene. That means that what they found and reported on were the facts as they saw them. It doesn't mean something different didn't happen." He ran his hands up her arms and cupped her cheeks. "Look. I will be totally honest. I believe the reports I've read. The fire investigator. The police report. The autopsy. But I struggle with some of the things your brother mentioned, which makes me wonder. So, I will use the resources I have to help you find answers. But I need to know you'll accept whatever we find. Good or bad."

"I can do that as long as I know your friends are looking into the matter without blinders on. That they are at least willing to consider that someone arranged my brother's death to look like something it's not."

"I can guarantee that they will do that. I just need you to trust me. Do you trust me?"

She raised up on her tiptoes, her lips scant centimeters from his. "Can I trust you with my life?"

❄

TRUST? DID SHE REALLY TRUST GARRET? ANYONE?

Thus far, most people she'd known in her life

destroyed her faith in them like pressing the delete key on a keyboard.

"My buddies and I will look at everything with an open mind. No pre-judgements based on what anyone is saying, but—"

"I know. If you find that he really did die as the autopsy said, then I have to accept it. It won't be easy, but as long as I know people are taking this seriously—"

"I wouldn't be here, nor would I have made the phone call if I didn't genuinely understand where you're coming from." Garret held her tight, but his hands caressed her muscles with a tenderness that she hadn't had in a long time.

If ever.

He had a way of making her feel desired. Wanted. Cared for.

Even when he'd first given her an odd look when she'd gone to him with her thoughts about her brother's death, he still seemed as though he cared.

And who spends their day putting on new doors and locks when he should have been sleeping after a twenty-four-hour shift?

Someone who either cares or wants to get into her pants.

Or both.

God, she really hoped it was both. Part of her might be using his body to help soothe the pain and shut out the images of what she thought her brother's last moments had been. However, the rest of her really enjoyed Garret's company. She loved that he took time to get to know her before even making a move and even then, he didn't expect anything from her at the end of their date. Who does that anymore?

"You did lock my front door, didn't you?" she asked, swallowing the nerves that had fluttered from her stomach to her throat.

He nodded, a smile spreading across his face, his fingers across her lower back.

She'd always been more than comfortable in her own skin, and she'd never been shy a day in her life. Even though her confidence stumbled a few times with Garret, she wanted him more than she'd wanted anything in a long time. "I thought maybe we could take a bottle of wine upstairs," she whispered. Her cheeks flushed, which was unusual for her when it came to men.

Not that she'd had a ton of men. Only a couple of long-term relationships, but none of them could ever call her bashful when it came to things that happened inside the bedroom.

Or other places for that matter.

"Wine? Upstairs?" The right side of his mouth lifted a little higher than the left. His brows twitched slightly, and his eyes grew wide.

A sudden pounding of her heart thumped in her chest. She pressed her hands on his shoulders with the intention of pushing away. Rejection wasn't something she did well. Normally her sarcasm came out and that never ended well, especially when it came to Garret. "I was just kidding."

"No, you weren't," he said with a gruff tone. "But if I had another drop of alcohol, I'd be asleep the second I lay down in your bed and that might not bode well for me." He arched a brow. "Or you."

She licked her lips as a warmth spread from under her skin, coating her body like soft lotion. "Yeah, I think I'd kind of like you awake." His pectoral muscles twitched when she slipped her hand under his shirt, letting her fingers glide through his soft chest hairs. Pressing her lips against his neck, just under his earlobe, she let out an audible sigh.

"Keep doing that and we won't make it to your bedroom."

Before she could take another breath, he lowered his head, slipping his tongue into her mouth. He tasted like a hint of cinnamon on warm sourdough bread. His hard body pressed against hers in a promise of what was to come.

A wave of insecurity gripped her mind. She wasn't sure if it came from the fact that it had been over a month since they had started hanging out. He'd kissed her quickly once, but it hadn't been as blatantly sexual as the way he molded his hands and body with hers. His hesitancy made her question her sexuality.

Her desirability.

And now, in the moment, she worried she wouldn't be enough to satisfy a man like Garret.

Swiftly, he unfastened her bra, drifting his large, callused hands to the underswell of her breasts, his thumbs fanning her tender skin just under her tight nipple.

She groaned from deep in her throat, letting it vibrate through her mouth, rattling her teeth. "Oh my," she managed when he pinched and tugged at her nipples before lifting her shirt up over her head, tossing it to the side.

Standing in her kitchen, topless, she took a step back as his gaze roamed up and down, smearing her body with the sizzle of a fire crackling in the distance. She looped her finger into her shorts, undoing the button.

"Upstairs," he said with a thick growl, tossing his own shirt to the side.

Trying not to giggle, she turned and raced out of the kitchen. His footsteps rattled the floor right behind her. By the time she'd pushed opened her bedroom door, she'd managed to kick out of her jean shorts.

When she turned to face him, she gasped, gawking at his naked body. He'd accomplished stripping down to nothing, except for holding his jeans in one hand. He fiddled with them, reaching into a pocket, pulling out his wallet.

Her nipples tightened into hard nubs and wetness lined her panties, spreading warmth across her skin.

His abs were chiseled with a clear six-pack. His long legs were lined with defined muscles.

And the rest of him?

She swallowed.

Hard.

He breezed past her, sending a sweet shiver up her spine as she gawked. He winked as he tossed his billfold on the nightstand. "We have a problem."

"Not from where I'm standing." She bit down on her fingernail, finding it impossible to tear her gaze away from his body. Specifically, from below the waist.

He laughed, wiggling his finger at her. “You have on more clothing than I do.”

She glanced down, staring at his fingers looping around the string of her thong, tugging them over her hips, his sweet lips kissing from her hips to her toes and back up.

“You’re beautiful,” he whispered, his tongue running over her lips. Closing her eyes, she gave in to whatever it was that Garret craved.

Normally, she liked to be controlling when it came to sex. She knew what she liked, and the few boyfriends she had never complained, though one taught her a few tricks.

Garret tenderly laid her on the bed after pulling back the sheets. His lips and hands roamed her body like the winds gently rustled the trees, swaying back and forth, tickling every leaf. He teased her by barely touching her, then plunging inside with his fingers or tongue. In minutes, he brought her so close to utter gratification, she thought she might convulse right off the bed.

But then he’d pull back, kissing her inner thigh, taunting her breasts, as if he knew exactly how her body would respond to every single touch, right down to how he breathed on her neck just below her earlobe.

Every time she reached for him, he batted her hands away and went back to giving her the kind of pleasure that she'd fantasized about.

Gripping the longer part of his hair, she arched her back, digging her ankles into the bed. "Garret, please," she begged as she lifted her hips, hoping he'd dig in a little deeper and circle her tight nub just a little harder.

"Oh God, yes," she panted out a moan as Garret made her body spasm. Her toes curled, and her calf muscles tightened. She blinked as the room blurred. She tried not to jerk, but she couldn't stop the violent release.

And he didn't stop.

He kept licking and stroking until she thought she might scream.

"Garret," she said, biting her lower lip, hoping to keep her screeching to a minimum. All her nerve endings cried out, demanding more and more.

He kissed her stomach, stopping at her belly button and circling it with his tongue.

Her body shivered again.

"I'm delighted you enjoyed that." He pressed his mouth over one of her nipples, sucking it, swirling his tongue over the hard nub before letting it pop out of his mouth, glancing up at her with a smile.

"Delighted is an understatement." She wiggled underneath him, curling her fingers around his shaft.

He growled, reaching toward the nightstand. "It's been a really long time for me, and honestly, I'm terrified if you keep doing that, that's how this will end."

"I'll make sure that doesn't happen."

As he rolled to his back, she took the condom from his hands and put her lips on the tip of him, taking him in slowly.

His fingers dug into her scalp as he gathered her hair. The way he touched her made her want to devour every inch of him, but instead she teased him with her tongue, gliding it up and down, staring up into his adoring, smoky eyes. His chest puffed out in a quick inhale, then lowered as he exhaled with a groan.

His soft skin tightened under her touch. Tearing open the condom, she rolled it over his shaft.

"Christ," he said with a throaty moan. He grabbed her hips as she rolled herself over him, taking him all in with purposeful motion.

She pressed her palms on his chest. Feeling him

inside her sent off tiny electric pulses from her toes to her throat. The faster she moved over him, the stronger the build-up. Digging her nails into his skin, she bit down on her lower lip, trying desperately to control her body before she exploded like a volcano.

But she did so in vain.

Garret reached up, cupping the back of her neck, drawing her mouth to his. Their tongues met in a wild frenzy as he pumped his release into her body with long, strong strokes.

His groans filled her mouth like he filled her body.

Collapsing to his chest, she tried to take in a deep breath. Her lungs burned, and her heart pounded erratically.

His strong, powerful hands ran up and down her back, gently massaging her shoulder blades. Their labored breathing filled the room like the mist from a hot steam.

He rolled her to the side, pulling the covers over them, and wrapped his arms around her body, kissing her cheek.

"You're not planning on sneaking out of here soon, are you?"

He laughed. "I do have to leave by five thirty. I have a meeting on base at seven."

"Don't leave without saying goodbye. I hate that." Actually, she didn't like to have men sleep in her bed. Even when she'd been in a relationship, she preferred to sleep alone.

But not with Garret.

What the hell did that mean?

She kissed his chest. It was a question she wasn't even going to consider. Instead, she snuggled up against him, closed her eyes, and for the first time in a long while, let herself relax.

CHAPTER 5

Garret hated waking Tabitha. She looked like an angel with the white sheet wrapped around her sexy, naked body. Her tanned skin glowed in the moonlight, and her raven hair covered her flawless face. She'd barely peeked her eyes open before reaching up and giving him a good morning kiss that had he not overslept, would have led to the best morning he'd had in a long time.

Though waking up next to her had been a good way to start the day.

Garret pushed open the doors to the station house on the base just a little before seven in the morning. Becca Rivers sat behind the big desk to the right and greeted him with a smile.

"How's the baby doing?" he asked.

"She's a daddy's girl, that's for sure." Becca had married Declan, a fellow senior firefighter less than a year ago. He missed working with her on the team, but after she had a baby, she opted to stay on administrative duty, versus going back to running into burning buildings. She currently worked as Ace'sassistant, and the station wouldn't run smoothly without her organizational expertise and her ability to keep everyone in line.

"I bet she's got Declan wrapped around her tiny little finger." Garret always enjoyed seeing his friends with their families. Watching their kids stumble around, learning how to walk, or ride a bike for the first time. He'd be lying if he didn't feel a pang of jealousy every time he went to a family barbeque.

Becca laughed, turning the frame on her desk around. "The latest picture says it all."

In the image, Declan held his daughter, kissing her chubby little cheeks, while her arms were wrapped around his neck with a big smile.

Out of the corner of Garret's eye, he saw Declan step from the conference room.

"I see my wife is showing off the cutest little girl in the world." Declan slapped Garret on the back before taking the frame in his own hands. "I do make good-looking kids."

"One kid and I think I might have had something to do with it." Becca snagged the picture and placed it back on her desk. "She does look just like her mother."

"But who does she call for in the middle of the night?" Declan asked with a grin.

"I trained her to do that," Becca said, laughing. "I swear, Garret, I think if Declan could, he'd breastfeed."

Garret burst out laughing, bending over, resting his hands on his knees. "That is an image I never needed in my head."

"Are you attacking my manhood, honey? At work, no less." Declan planted his hands on his hips.

She batted her thick eyelashes. "Not at all. I'm just letting our friend know what a great daddy you are."

"Good to know." Declan leaned over the desk, kissing his bride on the cheek.

Garret enjoyed the banter, but his mind kept wandering back to the woman he'd left this morning. Tabitha had been through the ringer the last couple of weeks, and now she was trusting him to help her find the truth behind her brother's death and the story he'd been working on.

Garret worried he wasn't up for the task.

"I'll see you in the conference room." Declan turned and headed back down the hallway.

Becca shook her head. "He's all ready to have another one."

"And what about you?" Garret asked.

"Oh, I want more. But I can wait another year. Just seeing Brodie and Harper with the twins is enough birth control anyone needs."

"Those two are rambunctious." Garret peered down the hallway, just as his phone buzzed. He pulled it out of his pocket and saw Fletch's number flash across his screen. "I've got to take this."

"Ace isn't here yet, so you've got time."

Garret nodded, stepping back outside. "Hey."

Fletch and his wife had lived down the street in Garret's hometown. When he'd gotten the bug to join the Air Force, Fletch had been a great source of information. He would have preferred Garret join the Army, but Fletch had been supportive, and Garret had always looked up to him as a father figure.

Fletch didn't like that much, balking that he

wasn't *that* much older, even though he had a good fifteen years on Garret.

"Do you have anything interesting for me?" Garret sat down on the stoop. The morning sun shone bright in the blue sky. Two fighter jets roared overhead, leaving a white trail behind.

"Depends on your definition of interesting. Turns out the cops first on the scene at the Moore party when Ashley died were the same officers that were the first to arrive at Steve's break-in. But that's not weird all by itself."

"No, it's not," Garret agreed.

"But Officer Riley was the first on the scene at Sandra Creeco's car crash. He was off duty and just happened to be passing by. He was injured in the rescue attempt. I did some digging, and it turns out he had some run-ins with the law as a juvenile, but he turned himself around in his early twenties after actually being arrested for assault with a deadly weapon."

"How'd he go from that to being a cop?"

"A diversion program and according to his old case manager, he's the poster child for voluntary systems. It's all about reducing harm and risk and creating better relationships between the police and the citizens."

"All aimed at developing trust." Garret had heard of such programs and believed them to be a better alternative than simply tossing people in jail. But it didn't always work. "What do you think about him? His record?"

"I'd say it's questionable. There are a few marks on his career, but nothing that stands out as a huge red flag."

"What about his partner? Officer Dani?"

"Boy next door type. On paper, those two are good guys. And based on the few people I got to talk to, exemplary cops, but Riley is a bit of a rebel and it should be noted that Riley is good friends with Assistant District Attorney Jeff Bellen's wife, Lisa."

"Why is that important?" Garret asked, rubbing his temple with his free hand. Too many players and nothing made sense.

"Besides being married to Ivan Moore's daughter?"

"Yeah."

"Not exactly sure, but I'm digging deeper."

Garret let the information settle in the corner of his brain. It still didn't add up to a conspiracy to kill Steve, but it did raise a few more red flags. "Anything else?"

"I'm sending a picture to your email. The image

is of Ashley and Steve, but there are some people in the image that I don't know who they are. Maybe your friend will recognize them and give me other places I can poke around."

"I'll be on the lookout."

"That's all I've got for now," Fletch said.

"Thanks, Fletch. Say hello to the family for me." Garret stuffed his phone in his back pocket just as his captain, Ace, pulled in.

Garret sat on the steps, letting out a long breath.

The only motive to kill Steve was wrapped up in Ashley, but so far, her death seemed to be an accident. That said, something scratched the back of Garret's mind. Nothing added up, but with three people dead who knew each other, that sent up more warning flags with a dozen more unanswered questions.

"You look constipated," Ace said with a slight chuckle as he joined Garret on the steps.

"My mind is all backed up."

Ace laughed harder. "Good retort. Now tell me why."

"My neighbor's dead brother."

"Ah, I see." Ace was ten years older than Garret and when he'd first joined the team, Ace had been his crew chief. Now, he ran the station, and Garret couldn't ask for a better boss.

Or a better friend.

"I hate to ask this, but you've got a buddy in IT, right?" Garret asked.

"Yeah. Ex-Navy SEAL, Tex. A good buddy of mine. Why?"

"I need someone to find out who an email address belongs to and maybe do some facial recognition magic. Tabitha's brother got a threatening email to back off a story—"

"Wait, back up one second." Ace stood. "I thought you'd gotten her to accept her brother died of an overdose and caused his own house fire?"

Garret shook his head. "I got her to understand if she's right, and she pushes the wrong buttons, she'll end up six feet under too."

"All right then. I'll get you Tex's contact information. If anyone can figure out where the email was set up, it's Tex. Now what about this facial recognition stuff?"

"I've got a buddy in Delta Force. He dug up a picture that has Steve, Tabitha's brother, and his ex-girlfriend, Ashley, the chick who died at Moore's house, in it, but he can't trace the other people.

Thought maybe Tabitha could, but if not, then maybe Tex can."

"I'm sure he can," Ace said.

"I appreciate the help." Garret took the hand Ace offered and followed him back through the doors to the station.

"So, you really like this woman, I hear."

"Yeah, she's cool," Garret said, trying to act nonchalant about how much Tabitha rocked his world.

"Oh boy. Do you have it bad," Ace said, slapping his back. "Why is it that everyone on my team has to fall hard and fast and with drama?"

CHAPTER 6

The last thing Tabitha wanted to do was show a house today. But she'd promised to stay out of trying to find out who had killed her brother. So, she might as well do what paid her bills.

She took the left into the driveway of an upscale home off Pineapple Avenue not far from the Causeway, stopping at the gate. Punching in the keycode, she waited for the gate to open. She pulled in, checking her rearview mirror, making sure the potential buyer followed her onto the property.

After parking in front of the detached three-car garage, Tabitha snagged her briefcase and stepped from her sport SUV. Normally, she liked to get to a house a few minutes before a client, but Julia Hickey had been early, and Tabitha later than she had intended. Since the house had been unoccupied for a few weeks now, she wasn't worried about the condition. It would be as she'd left it three days ago.

"I hope you weren't waiting long?" Tabitha stretched out her hand, taking Julia's in a firm shake. "There was an accident on the other side of the Causeway."

"Only about five minutes." Julia had long, blond hair that she had pulled back in a low ponytail. A gray streak lined the side of her head, but it blended nicely with her natural color. According to Julia, she and her husband were looking to downsize now that their children were grown and gone.

This particular listing, right on the Intracoastal, was three thousand square feet with a two-bedroom apartment over the detached garage. The owners were asking $749,000.

"I really like this area. Right now, we're living in a gated community in Palm Bay. It's beautiful, but the house is just too big, and I want to live on the water."

"You'll love the view. Why don't we go take a look?" Tabitha led the way, pointing out all the features on the outside. Once inside, she let Julia wander about. Tabitha had found that it was best to let the client touch, feel, and see for themselves, while occasionally pointing out the selling points they might have missed or seemed the most interested in.

Tabitha set her briefcase down on the kitchen counter before heading upstairs.

It took thirty minutes for Tabitha to show Julia the entire house. Julia acted as if this were the best house she'd ever laid eyes on, but Tabitha considered herself a good read of clients, and this house just didn't have the shiver factor for Julia.

"I really love the location and the view, but there are some things that need to be updated. How firm on price are the sellers?" Julia asked as she stepped from the back door.

Tabitha secured the lock, tucking the keys into her purse. "They have had some quotes on some of the needed updates, so I can tell you they are negotiable, but they wouldn't entertain an offer less than seven hundred and fifteen thousand."

"Good to know. I'll need to talk to my husband. He'll want to come and see it before we make an offer."

"You have my number. I do have three other people looking at the property this week, and I suspect it won't stay on the market too long." Tabitha wasn't lying, but it still sounded like a high-pressure sales pitch. "I'll call you if I get any real interest or an offer."

"I appreciate it. I've really got to run. Sorry." Julia slipped behind the steering wheel. She waved as she punched the gas, taking off down the driveway a little faster than Tabitha approved of.

She took in a deep breath, dropping her purse in the passenger seat. Tapping the brake, she hit the start button. The engine tripped twice before turning over, which was odd, but the car was getting older and perhaps it needed a new starter. She reached in the back for her briefcase. "Shit," she mumbled. Digging into her purse, she found the house keys and scurried off toward the back door. That briefcase not only had all her paperwork, but her brother's laptop, something she didn't want to leave behind.

She stuck the key in the lock and turned it.

Ka Boom!

Boom!

Pop!

Clutching her ears, she dropped to her knees, falling forward as heat spread across her skin. She glanced over her shoulder as black smoke billowed from her car. Pieces of metal dropped to the ground inches from her body.

Her thigh seared in pain, and she gasped when she looked down to see blood flowing from an open gash. Panic gripped her heart as she searched for her phone.

Only, she'd left it in her purse.

Which was in her burning car.

She pushed opened the door and stumbled across the tile floor. The ringing in her ears screamed like fingers on a chalkboard. She found the phone in the kitchen and hoped the owners hadn't canceled the service.

Her heart pulsed when she heard the buzz of a connection. She tapped 9-1-1 and crumpled to the floor.

❄

GARRET SAT IN THE BACK OF THE CONFERENCE ROOM with Zach on his right and Gunner on his left. Ace leaned against the windowsill while Hunter, the crew chief, went over the schedule for mandatory training along with shift changes while each team went through annual testing. The next month would be grueling with double shifts and fitness tests. But he'd been through it before.

He flipped his phone over, not only checking the

time, but looking to see if Tabitha had called or texted. He'd turned it to silent mode because Ace couldn't stand listening to anyone's phone vibrate on the table, but he never bitched about someone checking it. Half the men in the room had families, and today was technically a day off, so if someone had to step out and deal with a problem at home, both Ace and Hunter would understand.

Nothing.

She had mentioned something about showing a house this morning and meeting with her boss, but then she said she'd be working at home all day.

The sound of boots hitting the tile in rapid succession echoed down the hallway.

"Sorry to interrupt," Becca said as she skidded to a stop in the doorway.

"What's wrong?" Declan jumped up, racing to his wife's side.

"It's Garret's friend, Tabitha. Her car exploded—"

"Her what did what?" Garret pushed his chair back with such force it tumbled over. His stomach flipped as bile smacked the back of his throat.

Becca stepped forward, putting her hand on his biceps. "She wasn't in it, and yes, she's going to be fine. She asked the first responders to call us. She has a gash in her leg that needs stitches, and they are taking her to Whitten Hospital."

"Do you know what happened? How it happened? Cars don't just explode." His heart crashed into his ribcage. He ignored the tightness in his chest as he tried to take a deep breath. He pushed all his fears down into the pit of his gut and focused on what he could do.

And that was get to Tabitha.

"The call came in to the 9-1-1 center fifteen minutes ago, so I don't know anything."

Garret glanced toward Ace, who nodded. "We'll fill you in on the rest. Report back to me as soon as you can."

Becca and Declan stepped to the side.

Garret didn't look back as he ran from the station. His fingers fumbled as he yanked his keys from his pocket, hitting the button to unlock his truck. He did his best to keep to the speed limit as he navigated the streets toward the hospital just on the other side of the Causeway, nearly twenty-five minutes from the base. Twice, he pounded on his horn, and three times he slammed his fist on the steering wheel out of frustration, and he still had another five minutes before he'd be inside the hospital.

"Hey, Siri. Call Becca Rivers." It concerned him that no one had called him with any information.

The phone rang twice.

"Are you at the hospital?" Becca asked, not bothering to say hello.

"No. And Tabitha isn't answering her phone." He flipped his blinker on as he rolled to a stop three blocks shy of the emergency room parking lot. "Do you know who the first responders were? Who called you? I should have asked, but I was in too much of a hurry to—"

"Stop talking," Becca said with a hint of a laugh. "Peters from Fire Station #5 called me directly. His EMTs took her to the hospital."

"What about the cops?"

"I don't know who the police officers were, but I can find out."

"Do that. And if you don't mind, ask Peters to do us a solid and keep us in the loop."

"I've already asked him," Becca said. "The fire investigator has been called to examine the car."

"That's protocol." Cars generally didn't explode randomly. "Were you told where she was? How close to the car had she been?"

"All I know is that she called 9-1-1 from inside the house she'd been showing. Peters said she was alert and not injured other than the cut on her leg," Becca said with a reassuring tone. She was a couple years younger than Garret but had maturity and wisdom beyond her years. "He also said he'd call me if he found out anything at all."

"All right." Garret forced in a deep breath.

"And Garret. Don't go getting all overprotective like the rest of your buddies. It really isn't how to win over a woman. We pretty much hate overbearing, controlling men."

Garret laughed. "Because we know who wears the pants in your family."

The call went dead just as he parked. Shaking out his hands, he found his way through the waiting room and stopped at the window. "I'm looking for Tabitha Nelson."

"Yes. She's in exam room number three," the nurse said, pointing down the hall.

"Thanks." Garret rounded the corner with a tightness in his chest and a longing in his heart. He'd been tiptoeing around Tabitha since they'd first met. Their first few conversations he'd barely managed to keep from being tongue-tied.

And now that he'd slept with her?

He paused mid-step. Perspiration beaded across his hairline. Talk about being out of his league.

"Garret?" The sound of her sweet voice delighted his ears.

He pulled back the curtain. She lay on a hospital bed that had her torso tilted upright. A pillow had been placed under her knee, and a large bandage was wrapped around her thigh.

"Jesus," he whispered. "What the hell happened?" Carefully, he sat on the edge of the bed, rubbing his thumb under a small cut on her cheek.

"I don't know. I'm just glad I wasn't in the car when it blew up."

He leaned in and kissed her rosy lips. "Me too."

"Do you know anything? The police haven't been back to talk to me since the doctor stitched up my leg."

He swallowed, glancing down at her thigh. Blood soaked through the gauze. "All I know is that a fire investigator has been called in."

"Probably the same guy that ruled my brother's house fire accidental." She dropped her head back and sighed.

"It could be a different investigator, but Becca, Declan's wife, is going to get all that information for us." Gently, he squeezed her knee, leaving out that he'd rather it be Wesley, the same man who did the investigation of her brother's house fire. "Can you tell me what you remember?"

She threw her forearm over her eyes. "I said goodbye to my client. Got in my car and started it when I realized I had left my briefcase in the house. I got the keys, leaving my car running, and by the time I got to the back door, my car had exploded."

For some reason, he needed to see Tabitha's eyes. He lifted her arm and tilted her chin. "Had you met this client before?"

"No. She called me yesterday. Said she'd passed by the house and got my number from the listing."

"I assume you gave the police her contact information?"

Tabitha nodded. "You're a fireman. What would cause a car to blow up while it was just sitting in a driveway?"

"Nothing good." He knew exactly where her mind had gone, and he didn't see the point in trying to sugarcoat things, or worse, insult her by brushing his own fears under the table.

"Excuse me," a male voice said from the hallway. "How are you doing, Ms. Nelson?"

"Not great. Can you tell me anything more about what happened to my car, Officer?"

"You were first on the scene?" Garret asked as he stood, letting out a sigh of relief.

"Yes, I was. It's good to see you again," Rusty said.

"You two know each other?"

"Yes. I'm an old friend of Ace's, Garret's boss. Actually, we met when he pulled Ace's wife from a burning car, but that's a different story."

"What can you tell us?" Garret asked.

"Nothing yet about why the car exploded, but we did find out that Tabitha's client doesn't exist. We can't find anyone in the state of Florida with the name Julia Hickey."

CHAPTER 7

"You don't have to carry me." Tabitha laced her fingers behind Garret's neck. Her words might have been in protest, but the rest of her gladly let him lift her from his vehicle.

"The doctor said you should stay off that leg for a day or two." He hip-checked the truck door, adjusting her body in his arms. His keys dangled from his finger.

She glanced down the street. A couple neighbors stood in a driveway while their children played in the yard. "People are staring."

"I noticed. Those two are busybodies. I wouldn't be surprised if they either show up at my door in thirty minutes pretending to need something that can't wait until their husbands get home so they can try to figure out what's going on."

"I'm sure they can see my bandaged leg."

"Probably, but all they are focused on is the fact that my hand is dangerously close to your ass." He winked as he stepped onto the front stoop. "We should really give them something to talk about."

A slow burn tickled her lips. She blinked a few times, trying to break from his mesmerizing gaze. He held her eyes captive like a cobra preparing to strike.

"Kiss me. I dare you," he whispered, tilting his head.

"We'll be the talk of the neighborhood." She filled her lungs with a deep breath. The thumping of her heart echoed in her ears.

"I'm carrying you into my house. They're probably already thinking we've run off and gotten married."

"You did not just say that?" She bit down on her fingernail.

He groaned. "It's so sexy when you do that," he said with his mouth only an inch away.

In a daring move, she plucked her finger out of her mouth and palmed his cheek as she brushed her lips over his softly. It could barely be considered a kiss, but it sent blood rushing to those things that made her a woman.

"Can you unlock the door?" He rattled the keys. "So I can kiss you properly in private."

"You started this," she said with a laugh as she pushed the key into the door. "Suddenly shy?"

He laughed. "Something like that."

Once inside, he kicked the door closed and then quickly sat down on the sofa. His tongue darted into her mouth, swirling around hers, finding erogenous zones she didn't know existed.

He tugged his hand from her leg. A sharp pain shot up from her thigh to her brain. She tried to swallow her painful groan.

"Shit, I'm sorry," he whispered as he gently placed her on the sofa, tucking one of the pillows behind her back. Then another one under her knee. "I didn't mean to hurt you."

"It wasn't you. It just hurts when I move it."

"Then don't move it. I'll go get you some ice."

She hated to admit it, but she sure as hell could get used to this kind of treatment. She tilted her head and watched as his narrow hips swayed, and his tight ass twitched under his jeans with every step. She let out an audible sigh. When you looked up the definition of hot fireman in the dictionary, you'd find out that Garret Peirce would be the first example.

The only example.

"Are you hungry?" he asked as he strolled back into the living room, handing her an ice pack.

Placing it over her wound, she cringed. "I could eat something." She bit down on her fingernail. She knew walking would be painful and problematic. The realization that she would be dependent on Garret for help twisted her gut. It was one thing to enjoy the idea of being waited on, but an entirely different thing to need it.

And she didn't want Garret to feel obligated.

"I don't want you going to any trouble and really, you should have taken me home. I'll need to get myself set up in there, so I can take care of myself." The words tumbled out of her mouth. Her hands shook. Someone had killed her brother and now she believed without a doubt that the same person was after her.

Being alone wasn't an option.

"You're staying with me," he said with an authoritative and protective tone.

She arched a brow, her stomach doing a little roll as excitement lurched to every cell. But she had to stifle her desire and set some ground rules. At least for now. "I don't appreciate being told what to do like that."

"I don't think you should be alone," he said with a tight jaw.

"I don't either, but I'm not your responsibility, and you can't be with me twenty-four seven."

"My boss is getting coverage for my overnight shifts. The only thing I can't miss are my fitness tests and mandatory training, but both can be pushed to the last round and when I can't be with you, I can arrange to have one of my buddies—"

"Wow, in less than an hour, you've got this all figured out." She didn't know if she should be flattered or insulted.

Scared or excited.

Enraged or delighted.

He nodded. "You could have been killed today." He sat on the edge of the sofa. His strong hands cupped the sides of her face. "And I don't believe for one second your car had some mechanical malfunction, so until we know what happened and the culprit is behind bars, you're not ever to be alone."

She couldn't decide if she should kiss him to death for caring or smack him for being such a Neanderthal. The entire situation took her on a rollercoaster she'd rather not be on, and she liked the exhilarating ride. "Trust me, I understand that, and I appreciate everything you've done for me. Just don't tell me in that—"

"I'm sorry. I sounded like an asshole, and I could have worded all that differently, but I'm worried—"

She covered his mouth with the palm of her hand. "I'm scared. My brother is dead, and someone may have tried to kill me. I'm a proud woman. Fiercely independent. I've never needed a protector. That said, I'm not too stupid to live. I have no intention of being alone. I just don't like you telling me in that tone. Like I'm a child and not your girlfriend."

Shit.

Did that just come out of her mouth?

He cleared his throat. "First, I never meant to treat you like a child. When Becca came running into the conference room and told me your car had blown up, so many things went through my mind. I have never felt so hopeless before." He kissed her temple.

"And second?" she asked, wondering if she really wanted an answer.

"I like the idea of you being my girlfriend, for the record." He winked.

God, he was so adorable when he flirted.

Her cheeks heated. "I didn't mean to jump us

from one night to relationship status. I mean, I've been kind of a bitch to you since my brother died, and we really don't know each other. Probably should take things slow."

"You sure know how to cover a lot of ground in one sentence." He scratched the side of his face. "Yes. Slow. I like slow. And you weren't a bitch. I should have listened, and I didn't."

"I wouldn't have listened to me," she said, palming his cheek. There was so much she didn't know about him and so much she wanted to share. He had the kind of heart she knew she could love. The kind of man she wanted to love. "I know I didn't have anything to go on the night I came over here begging for your help."

He pressed his finger against her lips. "That's not the point. And you do now."

She adjusted her throbbing thigh, groaning.

"I'll let you rest while I make us some food."

"Wait." She tugged at his arm before he could stand and walk away. "Can I ask you something?"

"Sure."

Where to start? She had so many questions, both personal and professional. "Is it possible to make it look like a car explosion was an accident?"

"Truth?" He lowered his chin and arched a brow.

"Yes." She wanted nothing but the truth from Garret, even if it was something she didn't want to hear.

"Cars don't usually burst into flames like they do in the movies. Not even when they catch fire, so for yours to explode like that, well, something had to have made that happen. I got a text from Becca that said they have taken the car to forensics, so they are definitely looking for something."

"Like a bomb?"

"Exactly."

"Jesus," she muttered, swallowing the thick lump of fear that had formed in her throat. Her hands trembled. "So, we know then my car was tampered with while I was in that house."

He nodded. "Mind you, we have no proof of anything yet. But between the fact that Julia doesn't exist, and your car randomly exploding, which isn't really possible, Rusty is working on the idea that this is a potential attempted homi—"

"Please don't finish that statement." She shuddered at the thought of joining her brother in the afterlife. Steve had more than his share of hard knocks in his lifetime. He'd struggled in high school. Dropped out of college twice.

And yeah, he had done drugs.

But it had been three years and while there had been times Tabitha didn't trust that her brother was pulling it together.

This hadn't been one of those times.

"We're going to figure this out, and whoever did this to you, and your brother, are going to pay."

CHAPTER 8

Garret rubbed his temples. His eyes stung from staring at a computer screen, reading statements and reports over and over again for the last three hours. He'd come to a few big conclusions. The biggest one had been that whoever had tried to kill Tabitha today linked back to Moore's party. He clicked open the email from Fletch, staring at the picture of Steve and Ashley. He'd hoped the other couple had been Moore and his wife, or perhaps his daughter and her husband.

Who happened to be Assistant District Attorney Jeff Bellen.

But one couple he didn't recognize, and the other, their backs had been turned.

Tabitha, who sat across the table, let out an audible sigh.

"Are you comfortable?"

She had her leg stretched out across another chair, with a pillow under her foot and an ice pack placed over the bandage. He hated seeing her jaw tighten every time she moved, causing her more pain.

"I'm about as cozy as I'm gonna get after a piece of metal ripped through my thigh." She peered over the laptop she'd been working on, sporting a sarcastic grin. "I know you're just being thoughtful, but really, if I need something, I'll ask."

"This coming from the woman who told me how fiercely independent she was." He clicked his mouse, sending her an email with the picture. Hopefully, she'd know at least one of them.

"I am, but I kind of like watching you jump out of your seat whenever I feel like asking for something."

He quickly checked his phone. One text from Declan.

Declan: Wesley Armond is assisting with the

investigation into Tabitha's car. Ace says he's as trustworthy as Rusty, who has been named lead detective.

Garret: Thanks. I've asked my buddy Fletch to look into Officer Riley.

He laughed. "Don't get used to it. Once you're all healed, you'll go back to hosing down your own roses." He closed his computer, folding his arms over the top. "Because I really like the view."

She crumpled a piece of paper and tossed it, nailing him on the forehead. "I think I'll be putting up a fence."

The ease at which they had settled into flirty conversation surprised Garret. Even with his last girlfriend, he found himself with the jitters. As a kid, girls and boys teased him about his height. He'd always been so much taller than everyone else, and one kid dubbed him the Jolly Green Giant in sixth grade. He'd tried to laugh it off, but it had always made him feel like he was different from everyone else.

It carried over into his teenage years when girls started to think his height was sexy, and he wasn't quite sure what to do with the attention since he didn't feel comfortable in his own skin. The fact that he'd ran up to her bedroom, shedding his clothes without a care in the world had shocked him to the core. He knew women could be shy and concerned about their bodies. They were so much harder on each other in general than men.

But it was usually him dimming the lights and staying hidden under the sheets.

He snagged a beer from the fridge. He knew she wasn't taking the pain killers the hospital offered since she refused to fill the script, saying she couldn't stand the way they made her feel. "Would you like a beer or some wine?"

She leaned closer to the computer screen. "I might need something harder." She flipped the computer around. "That woman in the picture with my brother and Ashley was my client this morning."

"Are you sure?" He set the beer on the table, grabbing another one before sitting down next to her.

"Absolutely. That's her. But now her hair is a little longer, and she had a big, gray streak. She's got to be in her late fifties, early sixties, I would think."

"The man she's with appears to be older." Garret twisted the screen. "There are two other people in this image, but their backs are turned. Any idea where or when it was taken?"

"I don't know where. Nothing looks familiar, but based on my brother's bad haircut and the fact he's with Ashley, I'd say maybe four years ago." She leaned back in her chair, tucking a strand of hair behind her ear in a delicate motion. "I wasn't speaking to him much back then."

"Why not?" The one thing Garret really regretted was not paying more attention to her plea for help. Once he'd read the report, he'd been satisfied that her brother had large quantities of drugs in his system and that he'd been passed out and the fire overtook the house.

He'd seen it many times. Drug addicts burning candles, knocking them over while they shot up, or overdosed, the needle still hanging from their veins when first responders would show up, just like her brother. However, thinking back, the autopsy said Steve had died of an overdose. He didn't have smoke in his lungs because he hadn't breathed any in. The fire investigator, Wesley, had stated that the fire had been started in the bedroom. Steve died in the kitchen.

It was still possible that Steve had stumbled out of his bedroom, knocking over the candle without knowing it, or maybe the window had been open, and the wind knocked it over.

"Because of the drug use. He stole money from me a few times. But he'd been clean and sober for the last three years, and there was no sign of him falling off the wagon. He was gainfully employed and going after his dreams. I saw him a couple times a week, and I know he was going to meetings." She spoke with a slight tremble in her voice, but also the tone carried a sense of strength and pride.

He scooted closer, resting his hand on her back, rubbing up and down.

"I'm going to see if I can find Wesley's phone number so I can talk to him directly."

"Who is Wesley?" she asked, her lashes flickering over her questioning orbs.

"I don't know him well, but he used to be a firefighter with the Air Force. Now he's an investigator for the Fire Marshall. He was lead on your brother's fire."

"You know him?" She pushed back her chair and stood. "Fuck," she groaned, clutching her leg.

"Sit down," he said as softly as he could, pressing his hands on her hips.

"Don't touch me." She batted him away before letting her butt fall back on the chair. "I can't believe you didn't tell me you knew him. He could have very well covered up evidence that proves—"

"And he might have done his job. I read the report. I went over every detail along with the police report and the autopsy. That's quite the conspiracy theory to think all those people are involved in covering up a murder."

"My brother didn't accidentally overdose," she huffed under her breath. "I thought you believed me."

"Tabitha, I do. Something doesn't add up, but I think you're looking at this all wrong."

"What the hell does that mean?"

"You're assuming someone covered up something. That the police, or the investigator, or the medical examiner, or all three are guilty of conspiracy. But isn't it possible that someone pumped those drugs into your brother and then started the fire?" Gently, he placed the ice pack back on her leg. Kneeling, he took her chin between his thumb and forefinger. "Whatever happened the day Ashley died set this in motion. That's what we need to focus on. Who would want her dead and why? And what did your brother really know about it?"

She curled her fingers around his wrist.

"You're saying that it's possible that no one who handled my brother's case could be dirty?"

He shook his head. "Not what I'm saying at all. I have my doubts about the one cop, Riley. It seemed odd to me that he just happened to be driving by when Sandra's car burst into flames. And that's another thing. I was reading that report, and I am an expert in fires. The thing is, she crashed into a tree. There were no witnesses, and Riley said he didn't pass the accident until after the car had been burning hot, so how did he get hurt? I don't buy his story."

"You read his statement?" Her eyes went wide as she dropped her hands to her lap.

"I called in a favor."

"Why didn't you tell me you did that or any of this other stuff that has been floating around in your mind?"

He pulled up a chair, sitting as close as he could without having her on his lap. "Partly because I didn't want to worry you until I had more information. I've got friends digging into all of this."

"I want to be in the loop. I want to see everything. Be involved in every conversation. It's my brother who died, and I'm the one someone tried to kill today and—"

His phone rang.

"It's my boss, Ace. I'll put it on speaker." He tapped the phone, setting it next to the computer. "Hey, boss."

"I'll skip right to the point. Tabitha's car was rigged with a bomb."

She gasped, covering her mouth. "Sorry," she whispered.

"No need to be," Ace said.

Garret took her hand, hoping she didn't slap it away. Thankfully, she gripped it tighter.

"The trigger for the bomb was a timer, which was engaged the moment the car was turned on. Wesley estimates about five minutes."

"Not a lot of time for Julia, or whatever her name is, to get out of harm's way." Garret rolled his neck, trying to ease the tension.

"Well, we don't know her role in all of this yet," Ace said. "However, Wesley said, if Tabitha is willing to give him the information her brother collected, he would open up her brother's case file for re-examination of the fire. He has no control over the police department, unless he can find something and if he does—"

"Do you really trust this guy?" Tabitha interjected.

"I do," Ace said. "He was my crew chief for a year before he resigned from his post. He's a good man. He doesn't have much of a personality, but if I have to go running into a burning building with him, I know he'd have my back."

"And I trust Ace." Garret tossed in for good measure.

"I've got to run. My boys are running wild, and I promised the family a sunset boat ride. I'll have my phone, so reach out if you need to."

"Thanks, boss." Garret took his phone, ending the phone call. "I promise, I will keep you in the loop, but you have to trust me."

She nodded, but the sadness etched in her face didn't ease up.

"What do you need right now?"

"A sunset boat ride," she whispered.

CHAPTER 9

Sleep had eluded Tabitha. And if that wasn't bad enough, because of her tossing and turning, Garret hadn't got much shut-eye either.

Quietly, she rolled to her side. Based on Garret's deep breathing, she hoped he'd been able to fall back asleep. Her thigh throbbed with every beat of her heart. It hurt so bad during the night, it gave her a whopping headache. The dark night sky slowly turned a light blue, even though sunrise was a good hour or so away.

Tenderly, she put a little weight on her sore leg.

"Where do you think you're going?" Garret asked, pulling back the sheets.

She tried not to smile as her mid-section warmed as she stared at his bare chest and long legs.

He wore only a pair of loose boxers and how she wanted to get in them.

"To the bathroom." She glanced down at her tank top and her own boy shorts that she'd brought from her house when Garret had so kindly carried her across the yards. She could have taken pajamas that covered more, especially since she hadn't been up for anything sexual because of her injury.

If she were being totally honest, it wasn't just her leg that had kept her from sleeping well, but the man she lay next to all night. Inhaling his fresh musky scent that reminded her of sitting in a hot spring, smelling the rich outdoorsy aroma. His muscular frame holding her protectively, making her feel safe.

Cared for.

Even desired when his lips brushed against her temple right before he got out of bed to get her a glass of water or some Tylenol at two in the morning. He'd been so attentive, and never once tried to push her, where other men would have. It nearly brought tears to her eyes. For weeks before her brother died, she and Garret had begun to grow close, sharing long walks. They talked mostly about books, movies, and his buddies' kids.

"Let me help you." He stood, stretching his arms over his head and twisting his body.

It was impossible not to look him up and down, admiring his perfectly defined physique. Every muscle flexed and popped like a well-oiled machine.

"You're staring," he mused.

"Anyone ever tell you that you should be the cover of the firemen and puppies calendar?"

He shook his head as he curled his arm around her waist. "When I was little, kids used to tell me I belonged on a bag of vegetables."

She covered her mouth with her free hand as she hobbled toward the bathroom. "You were not called the Jolly Green Giant, were you?"

"Yep. Kind of hated that."

She gipped his biceps, turning to face him at the doorway to the bathroom. "Kids can be cruel. When I was in middle school, everyone used to ask me to crinkle my nose and make something disappear, usually the pimples on my face."

"That's really mean. I mean, seriously, Tabitha, the witch. So cruel."

"Yep. Kind of hated that." She chuckled, so happy he focused on the lesser of cruelties.

"I imagine you did." His thumb gently glided

across her cheek. "But you'd be beautiful to me even if you had a green nose with warts."

"That would match your green body."

Suddenly, his phone made a buzzing sound. She jerked, hitting her forehead against his nose.

"Fuck," he muttered.

"I didn't hit you that hard," she mused.

"It's not that." He held her by the biceps. "You okay on your own? I've got to answer that. It's a work S.O.S."

"Sure." She braced herself using the towel rack before closing the door. Running a hand through her hair, she tried to tame the bedhead. She turned on the faucet, splashing her face with cold water. Life had taken some strange twists. For years, she'd been afraid she'd lose her brother to a drug overdose.

There had been a time when it felt like she'd already lost her brother, so when he'd shown up on her doorstep, claiming sobriety, she practically slammed the door in his face. But over time, letting him into her life slowly, Steve had shown he'd truly changed.

Knock. Knock.

"Tabitha?"

"I'll be right out."

"I'd make it quick. We've got a problem."

She wiped her face dry before hobbling to the door. "What now?"

He looped his arm around her waist. "You're going to want to be sitting down for this."

"I really don't like the sound of that." She sat on the edge of the bed, swallowing the lump that seemed to never go away these days.

"Kelly Rines, the roommate of Sandra Creeco, was pulled from Indian River late last night."

"Jesus Christ. How many people have to die over...over..." she held her hands wide. "Over what?" She blinked a few times, tears filling her eyes. "It all goes back to Moore being accused of securities fraud, which had been dropped shortly after Ashley died in his house."

"You've never shown anyone the stuff on your brother's computer?"

She shook her head. "Just you and now your friends. But come on, all this killing over securities fraud?"

"You'd be surprised by the lengths some people will go to cover up even the smallest of crimes." He hiked up his jeans and pulled a shirt over his head. "Whoever is behind this, is afraid of what you might know and what is on that computer, and I don't think we're safe here anymore."

"What do you mean?"

"We're too close to your house. They could already be watching. Maybe they know you're in here with me, maybe they don't. But I can't take that chance."

"Now who's being a conspiracy theorist?"

"I said I wouldn't lie to you and that I'd keep you in the loop."

"Now you're scaring me."

"The ADA, Jeff Bellen, who is married to Moore's daughter Lisa has named you as a person of interest in the death of Kelly Rines."

"What?" She jumped from the bed, falling forward into his arms. "Goddamn it, that hurt."

"I'm sure it did."

"So what do I do?"

He helped her back to the bed. "Right now. We get dressed and head over to the marina where my crew chief, Hunter, has offered us his boat to stay on. Also, Rusty lives just down the street and Ace and his wife own the marina."

"That's convenient." She waved her hands in frustration. "I need to get more things from my house."

He tossed her cell phone on the bed next to her. "Remember the apps you downloaded for the security cameras?"

She glanced down, seeing the alerts that had popped up on her locked screen. "Shit."

"I'd like you to let me look at them."

"No problem." She touched her forefinger to the home key, unlocking the phone. "You think someone broke in?"

"I don't think that anymore. I know it." He held up her phone, showing a person, dressed in black, with a dark baseball cap covering their head, kicking in her door.

"Fuck. So now I'm running from the bad guys and the cops?"

"No. When they call you to either interview you, or question you, you'll go in with a friend of Claire's—"

"Who's Claire?"

"My crew chief's wife. Her friend is a lawyer. Until then, we're going to stay under the radar. Ace's buddy, Tex, is going to come up from Texas to look at the computer."

"This is fucking crazy." She tossed her hands wide. But what was she going to do? She certainly wasn't going to be a sitting duck. "I'm sorry I dragged you—"

"Nope." He waved his finger. "You did no such thing, and now you're just plain stuck with the giant." He wiggled his nose.

God. He had such a way of diffusing any situation, always making her smile.

Yeah. She had it bad for the hot fireman.

CHAPTER 10

"Hey, Rusty." Garret helped Tabitha into the booth of the diner a few blocks from the base. She seemed to be limping a little less, but her face still scrunched up in pain with every step.

"What can you tell us?" Garret asked, not wanting to beat around the bush. He waved to the waitress, who knew him, and pointed to the coffee mugs.

"Well, for starters we've gone from Kelly's passing being a suspicious death, to murder."

"Wonderful," Tabitha muttered.

Garret stretched his arm over the back of the booth, resting his hand on her shoulder, giving it a little squeeze. He hoped that would help ease her nerves.

"Oh, it gets worse. Jeff Bellen is up my ass. Turns out, Kelly wasn't just Sandra's roommate, but they both went to college with Jeff's wife." Rusty waved off the coffee when the waitress showed up with a fresh pot. "Coke, please."

"Who happens to be Moore's daughter who was also friends with Ashley who dated my brother for a short time." Tabitha folded her arms across her chest in disgust.

Things were starting to sound like six degrees of separation. "Any luck on finding out who Julia really was or who the other people in the picture are?" Garret had gotten a text from Fletch, saying he hadn't any luck with the image and Tex was in the air, on his way to Florida, so he didn't expect to hear from him until later.

"Actually, I'm glad you asked, because I do have something on that." Rusty pulled out a piece of paper from inside his sport coat. He spread it out over the table, turning the image toward Garret. "Tex was able to get me info before he got on his first flight. This guy, next to the woman you said was Julia. His name is Hickey Dawson. He's a known drug dealer for Rocco Tias and he works for Moore. Or should I say worked for Moore. He's currently in jail awaiting trial. I talked to him this morning and at first, he acted like he didn't know anyone or anything. But as it turns out, Julia is actually Emily Dawson."

"Wife? Sister?" Garret asked.

"Sister. I sent someone to her last known address. She's not there. But I'm not putting an APB out yet."

"And why not?" Garret asked with a little more venom than he had planned.

"Because of Bellen. First. He asked me not to, saying he had a reason that he couldn't let me in on yet. I find that odd. But Bellen has been acting strangely for a few years now, and he's twitching left and right over this last murder. I can't put a finger on what's up with Bellen. I've known him for years, and thought he was one of the good guys, but I have my doubts these days. For now, I want to keep him at arm's length during this for more than one reason." Rusty tapped the picture. "See this guy. That's Jeff. You can tell by the bald spot. But this woman, that's not his wife. That's actually Kelly, according to Hickey who also said they were having an affair right up until Kelly died. But Hickey also said Bellen is a player and had a brief affair with Ashley as well. Hickey said he'd seen them all the time in a corner somewhere, deep in conversation and that he'd seen them a few times in a parked car talking. Hickey is a bit fishy, so don't trust his intel yet. But I'm not liking where this is leading."

"Holy fuck, that's a mouthful." Garret rubbed his temples. "So, you think Bellen is tied up in these murders?"

"I'm trying like hell not to believe that. I'm going to try skirt around Bellen, but there is only so much I can keep from him. I need to check out some of Hickey's story. He told me that Moore had been pressuring his son-in-law to help make the criminal accusations go away, or he'd tell his daughter all about his affairs."

"This is all starting to make sense." Garret took a whiff of the bitter coffee. Best worst brew known to man. "But why kill off the women he was screwing and was he doing it with Sandra too?"

"Second question first." Rusty leaned forward. "Not according to Hickey. He can't say for sure, but he thinks she and Steve were killed more over the criminal accusations."

"But my brother and Ashley were really close. Even after they broke up. They knew they were toxic for each other and then when they both got off the drugs, they just decided to remain friends. It worked for them," Tabitha said, shifting and leaning closer to Garret. "My brother was pretty good with computers. He could have hidden things that I wouldn't find, but he knew me well enough to know that I would question if something happened to him. Maybe he knew about the affairs."

"Maybe he knew who killed Ashley," Garret said.

"Exactly what I'm thinking. Can you have your tech guy give me a shout tonight when he lands?" Rusty asked.

"Will do. What about interviewing Tabitha?" Garret asked. He didn't like the idea of her sitting anywhere in a police station being questioned for something she had nothing to do with, especially when she was the victim.

"I just did. Bellen does know I'm meeting with you. For now, I've got no reason to continue any line of questioning. He'll balk, but he can't do much right now without making himself look like he's hiding something." Rusty tossed a five on the table. "You two stay safe. I'll be in touch."

"This is a bad made for TV movie," Tabitha muttered. "My head hurts from thinking about all the moving parts."

"Mine too." He gave her a little nudge. "Let's get out of here. We'll pick up some groceries and head to the boat. We'll be safe there."

Garret pulled into the marina, parking next to Ace's SUV. "Stay in the car, I'll be right back."

"You promised you'd—"

"Leave the window rolled down. You can hear everything. I just don't want you putting any weight on your leg."

"I'm such an ass."

"No. But you've got a nice ass." He winked, snagging the computer from the back of the sedan.

"So do you," she whispered.

He did his best to keep from smiling as he approached Ace, who had rolled down the window. "You bring the goods?"

"Yeah." Garret handed Ace the computer.

"This is my buddy, Tex."

Garret leaned against the hood of the vehicle. The man in the passenger seat was older and looked like he'd seen his fair share of bad shit, but he had a softness in his eyes. "Nice to finally meet you."

"I heard you were instrumental ten years ago in saving Lexi's life."

Garret's cheeks heated. "Ace saved his wife. I just moved out of the way when bullets flew, letting Hunter take one for the team."

"I like this guy," Tex said, taking the computer and resting it on his leg. "A man has to have a sense of humor or life just sucks."

"I have to agree on that one," Garret said. "Tabitha thinks her brother might have hidden something on that computer."

"I'll find it. Don't you worry about that." Tex nodded, waving to Tabitha. "I think you should both know something. Bellen was interviewed a few years ago by the FBI. I haven't been able to find out why. My sources are being very tight-lipped."

"Can you speculate on what the FBI wanted with him?" Tabitha asked. "My brother thought maybe he helped squash the charges against his father-in-law."

"It very well could have been about that, but what makes me wonder if something else is going on is the fact that men and women I know well, aren't telling me. That means either they can't because it will jeopardize an operation or one of their agents, or they don't know."

"But you think it's the former." Garret glanced between Tabitha and Tex.

"I can't answer that. Bellen is married to the daughter of a man who has been under investigation for a few things, one being money laundering."

"We didn't know that," Garret said.

"Yeah. My brother said securities fraud."

"Well, laundering for Rocco Tias is one of the things I do know the FBI was looking into. I suspect that's why they've had their sights on Bellen. The question we have to ask ourselves, is Bellen one of the good guys, or one of the bad guys."

"My money is on the latter," Tabitha said.

And based on everything that had happened so far, Garret had to agree. But it seemed obvious that Tex had his doubts.

And so did Ace.

That gave Garret pause.

"Give me a couple of hours with this computer and let me talk to a few more people," Tex said.

"We'll be in touch." Ace gripped the gear shift, putting the truck in drive.

"Thanks, boss." Garret stood in the parking lot, watching as Ace pulled out onto the main road.

"Your boss seems like a really good guy."

"He's the best."

"How does he know Tex?" Tabitha asked, reaching her hand out, coiling her fingers around his biceps.

"Ace lived near him as a kid, and Tex helped him solve the murder of his high school sweetheart, along with everyone in her family."

"Shit. That's horrible."

"It was. Not only that, but the people that killed that family, nearly killed Ace's wife. Tex helped him find the killers and make sure they were put away for good."

"I think I like your friends." Tabitha pulled him toward the car. "I think I like you."

"Feeling is mutual. Now let's get you to the boat."

❄

"THIS ISN'T A BOAT, IT'S A FUCKING HOME THAT floats," Tabitha said.

Garret laughed as he set her down on the back bench. "It's a fifty-foot very expensive yacht, and by the way, Hunter and Claire are loaded. I mean, collectively, they have to be one of the richest couples in the state."

"I've heard of her foundation, but damn. This is real leather. I'm going to be a nosy bitch; where does the money come from?"

"Both families. They were high school sweethearts and what's really funny is that they were also step-siblings."

"That is oddly romantic and really weird." She

fluffed a soft pillow under her knee and stared out at the Intracoastal Waterway.

"Tell me about it," a deep voice vibrated against her ears.

She turned her head to see a handsome man with a stunning blonde with legs to die for on his arm.

"I wasn't very happy about her being my step-sister. Took me ten years to get over it." He helped the blonde onto the boat and stretched out his hand. "I'm Hunter. It's nice to finally meet you."

"Thank you so much for letting me stay here. You must be Claire." Tabitha smoothed down her shorts before tucking her hair behind her ears.

"Anything for this guy." Claire reached up and grabbed Garret's cheeks, shaking his head.

"You're worse than my mother," Garret mumbled, bending over and giving Claire a peck on the cheek. "Where are the kids?"

"Annabelle is over at her future husband's house," Claire said, shaking her head. "She and Jax's son, Rusty, have had this weird thing since the day they met, and I wouldn't be surprised if they did end up together."

"Let's just hope they will never be step-siblings," Garret said, laughing, but the joke didn't go over too well as both Claire and his crew chief gave him the evil eye. Garret shrugged. "I was kidding."

"We know," Claire said. "We just like giving you that look."

"You've got three kids, right?" Tabitha asked, moving her leg, making room for Claire to sit next to her while Hunter leaned against the side of the boat.

"We do. The other two are over at Ace's house. Dallas is four, and Ryder is one." Claire smiled. She had a genuineness about her that made it hard to believe that she was as loaded as Garret made them out to be.

Then again, her ass was on the finest leather known to man.

"Are you going to have any—"

"Nope," Hunter said, interrupting. "But when we dropped off Annabelle, Jax told us they are expecting another one." He held up four fingers, waggling them. "He's nuts."

"He's always got to outdo you, doesn't he?" Garret smiled, glancing in her direction.

She'd met all his single co-workers at his house, and she'd seen a few of the married ones in passing. But these weren't two men who worked together.

They were brothers in the truest sense of the word.

"We'll gladly let him win that one." Claire tipped her sunglasses up on top of her head. Her skin glowed in the late afternoon sky.

"Are you two all settled in?" Claire asked.

"We just got here. I've still got shit in the rental." Garret had a buddy take his truck back to his place and hang out in his house all night, just in case someone was watching. It made sense to Tabitha, and so far, they'd taken odd routes, stopping in odd places, and he didn't believe they'd been followed.

She, on the other hand, felt like there were a million eyes on her at every turn. Every time he turned the car on, she braced herself for an explosion.

"I'll help you unload," Hunter said. "You two ladies sit back and relax. We men will do the heavy lifting."

Claire waved her hand. "Go flex those muscles, babe."

"Does everyone on his team have a wicked sense of humor?" Tabitha asked, tilting her head, watching a very tall Garret strut next to a very broad Hunter.

"Yep. And they are all freaking eye candy. Wait till you meet my boys. They both look just like their father. I'll be beating the girls away with a stick."

Tabitha laughed. "Isn't it the girl you're supposed to be overprotective with?"

"You haven't met my Annabelle. She's got Hunter's stubborn streak and my tenacity. Doesn't matter how pretty she is, it's going to take a special man to tame that chick. Besides, we've really already married her off to Jax's son, Rusty. Cutest little bugger you ever did lay eyes on. And he's put some weird spell on Annabelle because whenever little Rusty is around, Annabelle actually behaves. It's amazing." Claire shifted, tucking her feet up under her butt. "I'm really sorry about your brother."

"Thanks."

A cool summer breeze kicked up, rippling the water. Birds flapped overhead, and a rumble of thunder rolled in from somewhere out at sea.

"You're in good hands with Garret, and the rest of the team has his back. Not a single minute will go by that someone won't be near. We've all been through some shit together. Hell, right here on this dock, Hunter took a bullet for Ace."

"Not the kind of stories you should be telling my girlfriend right about now," Garret said as he jumped on board. "And you weren't even there. I was."

"Oh, good Lord. I don't want to know anymore,"

Tabitha said, pointing over her shoulder. “Looks like we got a storm coming in.”

“You two batten down the hatches. I’ll be in touch.” Hunter took his wife’s hand and helped her off the boat.

“I bet they fight over who wears the pants in that family,” she mumbled, but not soft enough because Garret laughed.

CHAPTER 11

"The good news is that I don't think anyone will be coming out here tonight and bothering us." Garret lay in the big king-size bed with his ankles crossed and his fingers in Tabitha's hair while her head rested on his chest. He stared at the dark clouds threatening to let the water locked inside pelt the earth through the porthole from the bedroom to the main deck. The boat rocked with the wind, occasionally smashing against the wood planks of the dock. The Intracoastal was well-protected from large waves, but it didn't stop the wind from tossing even a boat this size around.

"And you call yourself a horror movie buff. This is exactly when the bad guys come with the machetes to chop up all the bodies and—"

"Are you trying to give us both nightmares?" He tugged gently at her silky strands. Everything about her was soft and sweet with just a bit of sass to keep a man on his feet.

"Right. Because either one of us is going to sleep well tonight? I wish that guy Tex could have stayed out here. He's a big badass dude even with one leg."

"It's best he's at Ace's, and they are both right up the street."

She rolled to her side, keeping her bad leg on top of her good one. Her long lashes flickered over her sensitive eyes. "Why haven't we heard from anyone?"

"Because there is nothing to tell. It's going to take time for Rusty to find Emily and corroborate Hickey's information. I bet by morning, with the help of Tex, they will have all the pieces put together."

"Are you trying to convince me? Or you?"

"Perhaps a little of both," he said. "How's your leg feeling?"

"It's a constant throb, but not as bad as yesterday."

He rolled, resting one hand on her hip. His other forearm was where she rested her pretty little head. She'd described herself as fiercely independent, and he had no doubt she was perfectly capable of taking care of herself. She was the kind of woman that needed no one and was wholly comfortable being on her own. That made Garret's heart pause. Could she be the kind of woman that would do forever? Did she really believe that there was one person she could let in for the rest of her life, understanding that it wasn't about taking care of her, but taking care of each other?

"You look so contemplative." She tapped her finger on his temple.

"My boss says this look makes me seem constipated."

She chuckled, but her face quickly turned serious. "What's going on?"

"What are we doing? I mean. Me and you. What is this? We went from zero to forty to zero to sixty faster than I can pull the hose from the truck."

She burst out laughing. "I can't believe you just said that." The bed shook as her belly laugh filled the cabin.

Talk about a bad word choice. "You know what I meant and what I'm asking."

"I know. I know." She waved her hand wildly in the air. Her laughter was cut short by a tap at the door.

That couldn't be good.

"I thought your buddies said they would call first?"

"They would." He pulled his phone from his back pocket. "Fuck. I've got a text from Rusty."

"What does it say?"

He crawled from the bed, opening the cabin door and moving into the kitchen where he could stand tall. "Jesus. He arrested Officer Riley. Someone came forward and said they saw him put something in the road right before Sandra crashed."

"Why come forward now?"

"I don't know. But he said that Bellen isn't answering his phone. No one can find him, and Riley is pointing the finger at Bellen for your brother's death."

"No fucking way."

Another tap at the door.

He pulled up Ace's contact information, sending him a quick text.

Garret: We've got company. I'm calling. Don't say anything, but be on the ready.

He tapped the number. Tossing the phone to Tabitha he mouthed, *don't hang up.*

"Who's there?" he called, putting his hand on the doorknob.

"It's Jeff Bellen. Open up. You're going to want to hear what I have to say."

He reached for Tabitha, who had taken a few steps back. He had to get them at least out on the deck, and not trapped in the cabin.

"Come on," he whispered. "Ace is listening. Don't worry. He's calling the cavalry."

She nodded.

"Step away from the door." Garret took the weapon he'd brought and tucked it in the back of his pants. Slowly, he pushed back the door, surprised to not only see Jeff, but his father-in-law, Ivan Moore.

He held his hands up in the air. "All I want is Steve's laptop. That's it. Hand it over and no one gets hurt."

"Are you threatening me, because that's an arrestable offense and doing so in front of the ADA, well that's not too smart."

"Don't be a wise guy," Bellen said. He stood near the dock, hands on his hips. "Just give him the computer."

"We don't have it." Garret kept Tabitha tucked

behind his back. Out of the corner of his eye, he saw movement in the marina.

Ace, no doubt.

"Don't fuck with me."

"We're not. We gave the computer to an IT specialist," Garret said, eyeing more movement in the parking lot. Perhaps he should now have Tabitha go back in the boat.

"I'm really sorry to hear that. Unfortunately, that computer was property of my firm. It's got sensitive information on it and in the wrong hands, well, that wouldn't be good," Ivan said with a smile.

"Honey, why don't you go inside." He patted her hip, then gave her a little push. The sound of her bare feet sliding across the deck dialed his pulse down a bit. Now all he had to do was keep these assholes from doing something stupid while he waited for Ace to pull an Ace from his sleeve.

He inwardly smiled at his own odd humor.

"I'm going to need that computer." Moore opened his suit coat, showing off his gun.

"Jesus Christ, Ivan. What the hell are you doing?" Bellen took a tentative step forward.

"Nothing. Just trying to get my property back."

"You can't threaten people. It would be criminal and I'd have to—"

"Oh, stop blustering. Like you're clean from any wrongdoing."

"You can't kill these people," Bellen said.

Garret wondered if he'd walked into a movie a half hour in. There was something in this conversation he was missing, but he hadn't yet figured it out.

Ivan laughed. "Me kill someone? Please. I'm a businessman. I'm just trying to get my property back without having to take someone to court."

"We don't have your computer," Garret said, glancing over his shoulder. Tabitha stood just behind the door with her arms wrapped around her middle. Her eyes wide with fear and filled with tears.

Garret needed to do something and do something quick. He reached behind his back, curling his fingers around the butt of his weapon.

"I wouldn't do that if I were you," Jeff said. "I need you to trust me."

"Why should he trust you? You're as corrupt as they come."

"That's funny coming from you," Jeff said, holding his hands in the air.

"You're the idiot that couldn't keep his dick in his pants." Moore slid his hand inside his coat, taking out his gun.

"But I didn't kill anyone," Bellen said with a

shaky tone. "You did. And for what? I told you I could bury that case, and I did. But no, you had to go running off killing everyone who knew anything. Or you thought knew something."

"What are you talking about?" Moore took his eyes off Garret and shifted his stance. "You killed them."

"No, he didn't," a female voice rang out from behind Garret.

He spun on his heels, yanking out his gun, but he quickly lowered it as he let out a puff of air, staring at Lisa Moore Bellen holding a weapon to Tabitha's head.

His heart nearly stopped. A tightness in his chest sucked the breath right out of him. Rage filled his veins.

No one threatened the woman he loved and got away with it.

❄

"I KILLED THOSE WOMEN. AND I KILLED THIS LITTLE bitch's brother."

Tabitha's teeth chattered as if she were as cold as ice when a woman stepped up behind her and grabbed her by the hair. She twisted and gasped when the butt end of a gun came down on the side of her head.

Garret lurched forward.

"Back off, asshole, or she dies," the woman said.

"You killed them?" Moore asked. His voice prickled Tabitha's ears, searing fear in her brain like a cattle prod.

She stared into Garret's rage-filled eye,. his gaze, and his weapon, shifting between Bellen, Moore, and the crazy woman holding a cold piece of metal to Tabitha's temple. Her head pounded worse than her aching thigh.

"I think the real question is why?" Garret asked, noting movement from one dock over. He had no idea how many people Ace could have gathered in ten minutes, but he was thankful for every single one of them.

"Yes, Lisa. Why don't you tell us why?"

"Why I killed those bitches? You really have to ask?" Lisa asked with a sneering laugh. "You mean besides the fact you were balling them?"

"Actually, I wasn't. But that's beside the point," Bellen said.

Tabitha tried to shift, taking weight off her bad leg, but Lisa grabbed her around the neck, squeezing her throat.

She coughed.

"Let her go," Garret said behind a clenched jaw.

"Like hell. If it wasn't for this bitch and her brother, we wouldn't even be standing here right now."

"I wouldn't go that far," Bellen muttered.

"What the fuck are you doing, Lisa? Come on, sweetie. Your husband can make this go away if you just put down the gun. I'm sure if you killed anyone, it was in self-defense."

Lisa laughed. "Oh, come now, Daddy. Wasn't it you who said that I should take what was mine and never put up with shit from anyone?"

"Yes, but that doesn't mean you should kill someone just because they were sleeping with your husband."

Lisa laughed. "I did kill Ashley and Kelly because they were fucking my husband. But I killed Sandra and Steve to save your sorry ass." Lisa pressed her forearm tighter around Tabitha's neck as she pointed her weapon at her father. "I had hoped I could pin everyone on my cheating husband. And, well, I still can. Unfortunately, Dad, if you don't help me, you'll die in the crossfire."

"Lisa. You're talking crazy," her father said. "We

can fix this." He took his weapon, holding it in the air. "Let's all just put down our weapons."

"It's too late for that, Dad. You're either on my side, or against me."

"Baby girl, I'm on your side."

"Then you take Garret's gun and shoot my husband. I'll shoot this bitch and then either one of us can shoot the fireman." She waggled the gun. "This is registered to my idiot husband. Stupid asshole. I can't believe my own father talked me into marrying you in the first place. Had you just gone into the family business—"

"Keep talking, Lisa," Bellen muttered, ripping open his shirt, showing off a wiretap.

"Fuck me, I didn't see that coming," Garret said.

Tabitha gasped as the boat rocked. Two officers stormed through the cabin cuddy, screaming for Lisa to put down the weapon.

Garret lurched forward.

Bang!

Tabitha screamed as she fell to the floor. Garret's body covering hers.

"Fuck," someone yelled.

The sound of boots clomping across the boat echoed through her brain. "Garret!" Panic gripped her soul as she clutched Garret's shoulders. Her ears rang as men shouted at one another. "Garret?"

"I'm fine," he whispered.

"But the gun shot?"

"Didn't hit me. I think it got Moore," he kissed her temple. "Are you okay?"

"No. No, I'm not. Not one bit," she said, biting back the tears.

"Shhh. It's going to be okay. It's all over now."

Tabitha buried her face in Garret's chest and let the tears flow. The sound of voices filled the air, but the only thing she focused on was the man holding her. Protecting her.

Taking care of her.

❄

GARRET PULLED TABITHA TO A SITTING POSITION, because he needed to see what the hell was going on around him. He held her close, tucking her head against his chest, stroking her soft hair, pressing his lips on her temple.

"You little bitch," Moore bellowed as he fell to the deck, clenching his shoulder. "You shot your own father."

"Get the fuck off me!" Lisa kicked and thrashed,

trying to break free from the cop who had her pinned down. "Don't you know who I am?"

"Yeah. A confessed murderer," the cop said.

"It's all him," Moore said, pointing to Bellen. "You have to arrest him too." Another cop knelt next to Moore, wrapping his wound, but not until after Moore had been secured with handcuffs. "I'm not going to jail alone."

"You're right. You're going to prison."

"So are you. I've got proof of your—"

"You've got nothing, and I've got immunity. I've been collecting shit on you for the last couple of years," Bellen said. "Now get my soon-to-be ex-wife and father-in-law out of here so these people can have some peace."

Garret nodded at his boss as he stopped just short of the boat. "How long have you been working on this?" he asked Bellen as he stepped aside while his wife spit on him.

Bellen wiped his face. "Since right before Ashley died. I took what I knew to my boss who took it to the Feds. Ever since then, I've barely been able to live with myself. I've had to do things I'm not proud of to take them down and for the record, I wasn't screwing any of those women. They were helping me. My biggest mistake was missing that the woman I thought I loved was a psychopath."

"That's got to suck," Garret said under his breath, though he regretted the second the words left his lips.

"You have no idea."

Garret helped Tabitha to her feet, checking her over for any other wounds.

"I didn't know for sure until Sandra was murdered that my wife had anything to do with it. I honestly thought that Rocco Tias had murdered Ashley. He'd been at the party that night and was pretty pissed at my father-in-law about me becoming an ADA. He didn't trust that I'd make sure any potential charges would be dropped."

"I guess he had reason not to trust you," Garret said, still eyeing the man. "But you put me, my team, and my girlfriend in danger tonight. You had no right to do that."

"No. I didn't. But the second I walked onto this dock, your captain knew what I was up to, and I did have the place surrounded."

Garret looked toward the dock, where Ace, Tex, and Hunter stood.

"I was about to fill you in, but you called me first, so we had to go with Bellen's plan."

"Can't say I'm too happy about being left in the dark," Garret said.

"Me either." Tabitha lifted her head. "I really didn't like have a gun touching my head. But what I really want to know is why my brother? Why did he have to die?"

Bellen stepped a little too close to Tabitha.

Garret pushed out his arm.

Bellen nodded, taking a step back. "I'm truly sorry he got caught up in all of this. I can't be sure until we do more investigating. But we believe Lisa killed him too. At least that is what Riley is telling us. And it was Riley who broke into your home. We've proven that with the images from your security cameras."

"That doesn't make me feel better."

"I know," Bellen said. "I wish myself, and the FBI, had handled this differently. I tried to warn Steve, but I don't think he realized what I was saying. Your brother was a good man."

"The email," Tabitha whispered. "But you didn't warn him. You threatened him." She took an aggressive step toward Bellen, but Garret quickly pulled her back.

"I couldn't show myself. I've invested three years of

my life trying to get enough on my father-in-law; I couldn't take the chance he would walk. I wanted Steve to back off so he didn't get killed because I hadn't gathered enough information, yet. But now, thanks to the two of you, I have what I need to make sure him, Lisa, Rocco, and all his cronies will rot in prison. I'm just sorry it meant the cost of so many lives."

"We helped too," Ace said, his arm looped over Tex, who stood next to Hunter, who had a big old grin.

"Hey, we helped too." Zach and Gunner came into view as they paddled through the water in a raft. "We made sure the cops got on the boat."

"All you did was watch." Garret let out a slight chuckle, holding Tabitha tıghter.

"I can't thank all of you enough," Jeff said, stepping from the boat. "I owe you all and hopefully someday, I will be able to repay you."

Garret ignored the chatter on the dock between his buddies and Bellen. All Garret cared about was the woman with her arms around his waist.

"You never answered my question about us," he said.

She glanced up at him. "Really? Now? You want an answer now?"

He nodded, smiling like a little boy going for his first ride in a fire truck.

"You asked for it."

For a brief second, he thought she might tell him to take a hike. But that thought ended when her tongue slipped between his lips.

He ignored the hooting and hollering of his buddies as he lifted her into his arms, carried her back into the cabin, and closed the door.

"Um. We're going to need a statement from the two of you," Bellen called.

"Oh, leave them alone. It's been a long night."

Garret didn't know who said the words, nor did he care. He set Tabitha down on the bed. "I think I might be falling pretty hard for you."

"Well, fall faster, because you're stuck with me now."

EPILOGUE

Six months later...

Garret paced in Tabitha's kitchen, gripping a set of papers between his fingers, waiting for Tabitha to finish her shower that she had to take after work. He shouldn't be surprised. She always did that.

But tonight needed to be different.

He hoped it would be special in a way his fiercely independent girlfriend would appreciate.

"My, my. What has you all jittery?" she asked as she brushed her hand against his chest before reaching for the glass of wine he'd poured just before she'd gone upstairs. She leaned against the counter, running her fingers through her thick wet hair. The mixture of coconut and the rich sent of a dark blackberry and bell peppers filled his nostrils, exciting not just his taste buds.

"You know I love you, right?"

She folded one arm over her middle while she arched a brow, sipping her wine. "And why are we asking such a silly question?"

"Because I have to make a decision that impacts you?" He'd meant his response to be not only sarcastic, but funny.

Only it hadn't come out that way.

"What decision is that?"

"My lease. It's up next month. I spend more than half my time here. But I'd be a dick if I thought I could just move in. But I don't know how to ask you if I should sign my lease or not."

"I think you just did." She set her glass on the counter and took the papers from his hands.

"And?"

"Are you asking to move in here with me?"

"I'm asking for more than that."

She dropped the papers. They floated to the floor like feathers, landing on the tile with a soft little bump. "What?"

"I want more than to be your roommate and share in the bills."

She cocked her head. "You mean you're willing to pay half my mortgage? Car payment? Credit card bills?"

"Why are you making this so hard?" He rubbed his hands over his thighs before digging into his right pocket, the ring tickling his index finger.

Tabitha wasn't a traditional woman. She didn't bend to tradition. He'd learned over the last six months that it wasn't that she didn't want to get married and have kids. It was more that she wanted to remain an individual. That while being someone's... no...his wife was fine. That being someone's mother would be special and amazing, but she refused to give up her own self. She wouldn't get lost in someone else's world.

And he didn't expect that of her.

But he sure as shit wanted to be married to her.

Have a family with her.

"Because I want to ask you to marry me, but I know if I dropped to one knee and pulled out this ring, you'd—"

She took the engagement ring from his hand and placed it on her finger. "I'd say yes."

"Are you saying yes?" He let out a puff of air while she bent over and picked up his lease papers from the floor and tore them up, tossing them in the air.

"I love you, you big goof. I want to have the world with you." She took her forefinger and wiggled her nose. "I wished for you to come to your senses and realize that while I like my independence, I love being with you. I love you."

"Thank God." He pulled her tight to her chest. "So, I have to be out next week."

"Well, we'll just have to have a garage sale and sell most of your furniture, except the dining room table and your bedroom set. Both are much nicer than mine."

"Ace says that the key to a happy marriage is just say, *yes, dear.*"

"I knew I liked that man." She looped her arms around his shoulders, clasping her fingers behind his neck. "I love you, Garret. You'll all I'll ever want."

"I love you, too." He pressed his lips against hers in a promise that meant more than any ring. Together, they could conquer anything.

Together, they would make their own footsteps in the sand.

Thank you for taking the time to read *Burning Bed.* I

hope you enjoyed reading it as much as I enjoyed writing it! Please feel free to leave an honest review!

Sign up for my Newsletter (https://dl.bookfunnel.com/rg8mx9lchy) *where she often gives away free books before publication.*

Join my private Facebook group (https://www.facebook.com/groups/191706547909047/) where she posts exclusive excerpts and discuss all things murder and love!

More Books by Jen Talty

ABOUT THE AUTHOR

Welcome to my World! I'm an Award-Winning and Bestselling Author of Romantic Suspense, Contemporary Romance, and Paranormal Romance. DARK WATER, book 2 in the NY STATE TROOPER series hit number 10 in Barnes and Nobel overall. THE BLIND DATE hit number 1 in the Contemporary Romance/Kindle Worlds List on Amazon. JANE DOE'S RETURN won both THE MOLLY and the BEACON before being published by the WILD ROSS PRESS.

I first started writing while carting my kids to one hockey rink after the other, averaging 170 games per year between 3 kids in 2 countries and 5 states. My first book, IN TWO WEEKS was originally published in 2007. In 2010 I helped form a publishing company (Cool Gus Publishing) with NY Times Bestselling Author Bob Mayer where I ran the technical side of the business through 2016.

I'm currently enjoying the next phase of my life... the empty NESTER! My husband and I spend our winters in Jupiter, Florida and our summers in Rochester, NY. We have three amazing children who have all gone off to carve out their places in the world, while I continue to craft stories that I hope will make you readers feel good and put a smile on your face.

To learn more about me please visit my website: jentalty.com

Sign up for my Newsletter (https://dl.bookfunnel.com/rg8mx9lchy) *where she often gives away free books before publication.*

Join my private Facebook group (https://www.facebook.com/groups/1917065479090470/) where she posts exclusive excerpts and discuss all things murder and love!

ALSO BY JEN TALTY

SPECIAL FORCES: OPERATION ALPHA: FIRE PROTECTION SPECIALISTS

Burning Desire

Burning Kiss

Burning Skies

Burning Lies

Burning Heart

The New York State Trooper Series

In Two Weeks

Dark Water

Deadly Secrets

Murder in Paradise Bay

To Protect His Own

Deadly Seduction

When a Stranger Calls

Federal Investigator Series

Jane Doe's Return

The Butterfly Murders

THE MEN OF THEIF LAKE

Rekindled

THE OMEGA TEAM: THE SARICH BROTHERS

The Lighthouse

Her Last Hope

The Last Flight

The Phoenix Agency: The Raven Sisters

The Lost Sister

The Lost Solider

The Brotherhood Protectors: Out Of The Wild

Rough Justice

Paranormal Dating Agency

The Blind Date

Spring Fling

Sassy Ever After

Lady Sass

All That Sass

There are many more books in this fan fiction world than listed here, for an up-to-date list go to www.AcesPress.com

You can also visit our Amazon page at: http://www.amazon.com/author/operationalpha

Special Forces: Operation Alpha World

Denise Agnew: Dangerous to Hold
Shauna Allen: Awakening Aubrey
Shauna Allen: Defending Danielle
Shauna Allen: Rescuing Rebekah
Shauna Allen: Saving Scarlett
Shauna Allen: Saving Grace
Brynne Asher: Blackburn
Jennifer Becker: Hiding Catherine
Julia Bright: Saving Lorelei
Julia Bright: Rescuing Amy
Victoria Bright: Surviving Savage
Victoria Bright: Going Ghost
Victoria Bright: Jostling Joker
Cara Carnes: Protecting Mari
Kendra Mei Chailyn: Beast
Kendra Mei Chailyn: Barbie

Kendra Mei Chailyn : Pitbull
Melissa Kay Clarke: Rescuing Annabeth
Melissa Kay Clarke: Safeguarding Miley
Samantha A. Cole: Handling Haven
Samantha A. Cole: Cheating the Devil
Sue Coletta: Hacked
Melissa Combs: Gallant
KaLyn Cooper: Rescuing Melina
Liz Crowe: Marking Mariah
Jordan Dane: Redemption for Avery
Jordan Dane: Fiona's Salvation
Riley Edwards: Protecting Olivia
Riley Edwards: Redeeming Violet
Riley Edwards, Recovering Ivy
Nicole Flockton: Protecting Maria
Nicole Flockton: Guarding Erin
Nicole Flockton: Guarding Suzie
Nicole Flockton: Guarding Brielle
Casey Hagen: Shielding Nebraska
Casey Hagen: Shielding Harlow
Casey Hagen: Shielding Josie
Casey Hagen: Shielding Blair
Desiree Holt: Protecting Maddie
Kathy Ivan: Saving Sarah
Kathy Ivan: Saving Savannah

Kathy Ivan: Saving Stephanie
Jesse Jacobson: Protecting Honor
Jesse Jacobson: Fighting for Honor
Jesse Jacobson: Defending Honor
Jesse Jacobson: Summer Breeze
Silver James: Rescue Moon
Silver James: SEAL Moon
Silver James: Assassin's Moon
Silver James: Under the Assassin's Moon
Becca Jameson: Saving Sofia
Kate Kinsley: Protecting Ava
Heather Long: Securing Arizona
Heather Long: Guarding Gertrude
Heather Long: Protecting Pilar
Heather Long: Covering Coco
Gennita Low: No Protection
Kirsten Lynn: Joining Forces for Jesse
Margaret Madigan: Bang for the Buck
Margaret Madigan: Buck the System
Margaret Madigan: Jungle Buck
Margaret Madigan: December Chill
Rachel McNeely: The SEAL's Surprise Baby
Rachel McNeely: The SEAL's Surprise Bride
Rachel McNeely: The SEAL's Surprise Twin
KD Michaels: Saving Laura

KD Michaels: Protecting Shane
KD Michaels: Avenging Angels
Wren Michaels: The Fox & The Hound
Wren Michaels: The Fox & The Hound 2
Wren Michaels: Shadow of Doubt
Wren Michaels: Shift of Fate
Wren Michaels: Steeling His Heart
Kat Mizera: Protecting Bobbi
Mary B Moore: Force Protection
LeTeisha Newton: Protecting Butterfly
LeTeisha Newton: Protecting Goddess
LeTeisha Newton: Protecting Vixen
LeTeisha Newton: Protecting Heartbeat
MJ Nightingale: Protecting Beauty
MJ Nightingale: Betting on Benny
MJ Nightingale: Protecting Secrets
Sarah O'Rourke: Saving Liberty
Debra Parmley: Protecting Pippa
Lainey Reese: Protecting New York
Jenika Snow: Protecting Lily
Jen Talty: Burning Desire
Jen Talty: Burning Kiss
Jen Talty: Burning Skies
Jen Talty: Burning Lies
Jen Talty: Burning Heart

Megan Vernon: Protecting Us

Megan Vernon: Protecting Earth

Fire and Police: Operation Alpha World

KaLyn Cooper: Justice for Gwen

Aspen Drake: Sheltering Emma

As you know, this book included at least one character from Susan Stoker's books. To check out more, see below.

Delta Force Heroes Series

Rescuing Rayne (FREE!)
Rescuing Aimee (novella)
Rescuing Emily
Rescuing Harley
Marrying Emily
Rescuing Kassie
Rescuing Bryn
Rescuing Casey
Rescuing Sadie
Rescuing Wendy
Rescuing Mary (Oct 2018)
Rescuing Macie (April 2019)

Badge of Honor: Texas Heroes Series

Justice for Mackenzie (FREE!)
Justice for Mickie
Justice for Corrie
Justice for Laine (novella)
Shelter for Elizabeth
Justice for Boone

Shelter for Adeline

Shelter for Sophie

Justice for Erin

Justice for Milena

Shelter for Blythe

Justice for Hope

Shelter for Quinn (Feb 2019)

Shelter for Koren (June 2019)

Shelter for Penelope (Oct 2019)

SEAL of Protection Series

Protecting Caroline (FREE!)

Protecting Alabama

Protecting Fiona

Marrying Caroline (novella)

Protecting Summer

Protecting Cheyenne

Protecting Jessyka

Protecting Julie (novella)

Protecting Melody

Protecting the Future

Protecting Kiera (novella)

Protecting Dakota

SEAL of Protection: Legacy Series

Securing Caite (Jan 2019)

Securing Sidney (May 2019)

Securing Piper (Sept 2019)

Securing Zoey (TBA)

Securing Avery (TBA)

Securing Kalee (TBA)

New York Times, *USA Today* and *Wall Street Journal* Bestselling Author Susan Stoker has a heart as big as the state of Texas where she lives, but this all American girl has also spent the last fourteen years living in Missouri, California, Colorado, and Indiana. She's married to a retired Army man who now gets to follow *her* around the country.

She debuted her first series in 2014 and quickly followed that up with the SEAL of Protection Series, which solidified her love of writing and creating stories readers can get lost in.

If you enjoyed this book, or any book, please consider leaving a review. It's appreciated by authors more than you'll know.

www.stokeraces.com

www.AcesPress.com

susan@stokeraces.com